DATE DUE

ANTROBUS COMPLETE

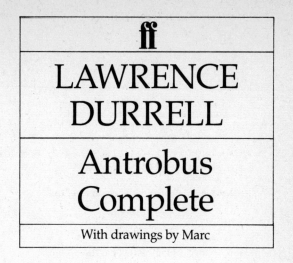

ff

LAWRENCE DURRELL

Antrobus Complete

With drawings by Marc

faber and faber
LONDON · BOSTON

This collection first published in 1985
by Faber and Faber Limited
3 Queen Square London WC1N 3AU
Reprinted 1986

Phototypeset by Wilmaset Birkenhead Merseyside
Printed in Great Britain by
Butler & Tanner Ltd Frome Somerset

British Library Cataloguing in Publication Data

Durrell, Lawrence
Antrobus complete.
I. Title
823'.912[F]   PR6007.U76

ISBN 0–571–13602–8

Library of Congress Cataloging in Publication Data

Durrell, Lawrence.
Antrobus complete.
I. Title.
PR6007.U76A83   1985   823'.912   85–6995
ISBN 0–571–13602–8

CONTENTS

ACKNOWLEDGEMENTS

Grateful acknowledgement is made to the editors of the following newspapers, journals and magazines in which some of the stories in this collection first appeared: *Lilliput* for 'La Valise'; the *New Statesman* for 'Cry Wolf'; the *Sunday Times* for 'Stiff Upper Lip', 'Something à la Carte?', 'The Unspeakable Attaché', 'The Game's the Thing', 'If Garlic be the Food of Love', 'Where the Bee Sucks' and 'The Iron Hand'; *Playboy* and the *Weekend Telegraph* for 'Sauve Qui Peut' and 'A Corking Evening'; *Mademoiselle* for 'What-Ho on the Rialto!'; *Mademoiselle* and *Harper's Bazaar* for 'High Barbary'; the *Saturday Evening Post* and *Town* for 'The Little Affair in Paris'; *Playboy* for 'All to Scale'; *Argosy* for 'Aunt Norah'; *Blackwood's Magazine* for 'Smoke, the Embassy Cat'.

THE GHOST TRAIN

I like Antrobus. I can't really say why – I think it is because he takes everything so frightfully seriously. He is portentious – always dropping into a whisper, clicking his tongue, making a po-face, pursing his lips, turning the palms of his hand outwards and making 'what-would-you' gestures.

We've served together in a number of foreign capitals, he as a regular of the career, I as a contract officer: which explains why he is now a heavily padded senior in Southern while I am an impoverished writer. Nevertheless, whenever I'm in London he gives me lunch at his club and we talk about the past – those happy days passed in foreign capitals 'lying abroad' for our country.

'The Ghost Train episode,' said Antrobus, 'was a bit before your time. I only mention it because I can think of nothing which illustrates the peculiar hazards of Diplomatic Life so well. In fact it throws them into Stark Relief.

'Every nation has its particular *idée fixe*. For the Yugoslavs it is trains. Nothing can compare for breathtaking romance with the railway train. Railway engines have to be put under armed guard when not in motion or they would be poked to pieces by the enquiring peasantry. No other object arouses the concupiscence of the Serb like a train. They drool over it, old boy, positively drool. *Ils bavent*.

'You twig this the minute you alight from the Orient Express at Belgrade because there is something queer about the station building itself. It leans to one side. It is neatly cracked from platform level to clock-tower. Moreover there are several distinct sets of ruts in the concrete of the platform which are highly suggestive. The first porter you engage will clear up the mystery.

Apparently every fifteenth train or so leaps the buffers, grinds across the Freight Section and buries itself in the booking office. No one is ever hurt and the whole town joyfully bands together to dig the engine out. Everyone is rather proud of this particular idiosyncrasy. It is part of the Serbian way of life.

'Well, being aware of this as I was, I could not help being a bit concerned when Nimic in the Protocol hinted that the Diplomatic Corps was to be sent to Zagreb for Liberation Day in a special train which would prove once and for all that the much-vaunted Yugoslav heavy industry was capable of producing machinery every bit as good as the degenerate Capitalist West. This tip was accompanied by dark looks and winks and all efforts to probe the mystery further proved vain. A veil of secrecy (one of the seven veils of Communist diplomacy) was drawn over the subject. Naturally we in the Corps were interested, while those who had served for some time in the Balkans were perturbed. "*Mon Dieu,*" said Du Bellay the French Minister gravely, "*si ces animaux veulent jouer aux locos avec le Corps Diplomatique . . .*" He was voicing the Unspoken Thoughts of many of us.

'There was no further information forthcoming about the Ghost Train as we jokingly called it, so we sat back and waited for Liberation Day. Sure enough the customary fat white envelope appeared ten days before from the Protocol. I opened mine with a troubled curiosity. It announced that the Corps would be travelling by a Special Train which would be placed at its disposal. The train itself was called "The Liberation-Celebration Machine".

'Even Polk-Mowbray looked a bit grave. "What sort of Devil-Car do you think it will be?" he said apprehensively. I couldn't enlighten him, alas. "It's probably a chain-drive Trojan with some carriages built around it in plywood."

'There was a short-lived movement among the Corps to go by road instead and thus sidestep the "Liberation-Celebration Machine" but the Doyen put his foot down. Such a defection would constitute a grave slight. The Yugoslav heavy industry would be hurt by our refusal to allow it to unveil the marvels of modern science to us. Reluctantly we all accepted. "Butch" Benbow, the naval attaché, who was clairvoyant and who dabbled in astrology, took the omens. Apparently they were not propitious. "All I can see is clouds of smoke," he said hoarsely, looking up from the progressed chart on his desk. "And someone gets a severe scalp wound – probably you, sir."

'Polk-Mowbray started. "Now, look here," he said, "let's have no alarm and despondency on this one. If the Yugoslav heavy industry gives me even a trifling scalp wound I'll see that there is an International Incident over it."

'The day drew inexorably nearer. The Special Train, we learned, was to be met in a siding just outside Belgrade. There is a small station there, the name of which I forget. Here at the appointed time, which was dusk, we duly presented ourselves in full *tenue*. There were to be flowers and speeches by representatives of the Yugoslav Heavy Industry. Most of the representatives looked nearly as heavy as their industry. But I couldn't take my eyes off the train.

'I'm not saying it was gaudy. It was absolutely breathtaking. The three long coaches were made of painted and carved timber; flowers, birds, liberation heroes, *cache-sexes*, emblematic devices, post-horns – everything you can imagine, all carved and painted according to the peasant fancy. The general effect was that of a Sicilian market-cart with painted and carved side-boards – or the poop of some seventeenth-century galleon. Every blacksmith, wheelwright and cartwright in Serbia must have had a hand in it. "*C'est un chalet Tyroléan ou quoi?*" I heard Du Bellay say under his breath. His scepticism was shared by us all.

'We entered and found our reserved carriages which seemed normal enough. The band played. We accepted a wreath or two. Then we set off in the darkness to the braying of donkeys and cocks and the rasping of trombones. We were off across the rolling Serbian plains.

'Two things were immediately obvious. All this elaborate woodwork squeaked and groaned calamitously, ear-splittingly. How were we to get any sleep? But more serious still was the angle of inclination of the second coach with the Heads of Mission in it. It was about thirty degrees out of centre and was only, it seemed, held upright by the one immediately before and behind it. It was clear that the Yugoslav heavy industry had mislaid its spirit-level while it was under construction. People who looked out of the windows on one side had the illusion that the ground was coming up to hit them. I paid Polk-Mowbray a visit to see if he was all right and found him looking rather pale, and drawn up on the higher elevation of the coach like someone on a sinking ship. The noise was so great that we couldn't speak – we had to shout: "My God," I heard him cry out, "what is to become of us all?" It was a little difficult to say. We were now gathering speed. The engine was a very old one. It had been abandoned before the war by an American film company and the Yugoslavs had tied it together with wire. Its gaping furnace, which was white hot, was being passionately fed by some very hairy men in cloth caps who looked like Dostoevsky's publishers. It seemed to me that the situation had never looked graver. Despite its age, however, it had managed to whip up a good forty-five. And every five hundred yards its would groan and void a bucketful of white clinker into the night which set fire to the grass on either side of the track. From far off we must have looked like an approaching forest fire.

'Another feature of the "Liberation-Celebration Machine" was an ingenious form of central heating which could not be turned off, and as none of the windows opened, the temperature inside the coaches rapidly mounted into the hundreds. People were fanning themselves with their tall hats. Old man, never have I seen the Corps subjected to such a strain. Sleep was impossible. The lights would not turn off. The wash basins appeared to empty into each other. And all the time we had the ghastly thought of all the Heads of Mission in the Hanging Coach, drinking brandy and gibbering with fright as we sped onwards through the night.

'The chance of some frightful accident taking place was far from remote and consequently nobody was able to relax. We did not even dare to get into pyjamas but sat about in that infernal racket staring desperately at one another and starting at every regurgitation of the engine, every shiver and squeak of the coaches. The American Ambassador was so overcome that he spent the night singing "Nearer My God To Thee". Some said that he had had the forethought to take a case of rye into his

The Ghost Train

compartment with him. Madame Fawzia, the Egyptian Ambassadress, spent the night on the floor of her compartment deep in
prayer. I simply did not dare to think of Polk-Mowbray. From
time to time when the wind changed the whole train was
enveloped in a cloud of rich dense smoke containing fragments
of half-digested coal the size of hailstones. But still the ghoulish
crew in the engine-cab plied their grisly shovels and on we sped
with mournful shrieks and belches.

'At two in the morning there was a ghastly rending noise as
we entered the station of Slopsy Blob, named after the famous
Independence fighter. The Hanging Coach somehow got itself
engaged with the tin dado which ran along the roof of the station
and ripped it off as clean as a whistle, by the same token almost
decapitating one of the drivers. The noise was appalling and the
whole Corps let out a unified shriek of terror. I have never heard
diplomats scream like that before or since – and I never want to.
A lot of cherubs and floral devices were ripped off the Hanging
Coach in the encounter and the people in the rear coaches found
themselves assailed by a hail of coloured fragments of wood
which made them shriek the louder. It was all over in a moment.

'Then we were out in the night once more racing across the
dark plain, the brothers Karamazov still plying the engine with
might and main. It is possible that, in the manner of Serbs, they
had heard nothing. We spent the rest of the night in Sleepless
Vigil, old man. The guardian angel of the Yugoslav Heavy
Industry must have been with us for nothing much worse
happened. But it was a pretty dispirited and shaken Dip Corps
that was finally dragged into Zagreb Station on that Liberation
morning. I can tell you, never was liberation so much in the
forefront of everyone's thoughts.

'It must have been about six o'clock when we stormed into
Zagreb squealing and blowing out an Etna of steam. The brakes
had been applied some three miles outside the station and their
ear-splitting racket had to be heard to be believed.

'But this was not the end. Though we missed the red carpet by
a quarter of a mile, and though the waiting dignitaries and the
Zagreb Traction and Haulage Workers' Band padded down the
platform after us our troubles were not yet at an end. It was

found that the doors of the coaches on the platform side were fast shut and could not be opened. I suppose Zagreb Station must have been on the opposite side of the track from Belgrade Station and consequently nobody dreamed that we should need more than one exit from the train. It was, of course, fearfully humiliating. We leaned against the windows making inarticulate gestures of goodwill and vague grimaces in the direction of the Traction Haulage Workers' Band and the Liberation Reception Committee.

'We must have looked like a colony of dispossessed fairground apes pining for the old life of the trees. After a good deal of mopping and moving there was nothing for it but to climb out of the Zagreb Flyer on to the permanent way and walk round the train to the reception point. This we somewhat shamefacedly did. But when all was said and done it was good to feel terra firma under our feet once more. Drawn up in order of precedence on Zagreb platform we submitted to the Liberation anthem sung by the Partisan choir in a register so low that it could not drown the merry cries of self-congratulation with which the Karamazov brothers were greeting the morn. Their observations were punctuated by blasts of hot steam and whiffs of sound from the whistle of the Liberation-Celebration Machine which looked even more improbable in the cold morning light than it had done the evening before.

'All this went off as well as such things can be expected to do; but sleepy as we were a sudden chill struck our hearts at a phrase in the Speech of Welcome which plainly indicated that the authorities were expecting us to make the return journey in the Liberation-Celebration Machine on the following day. This gave us all food for thought. Madame Fawzia made an involuntary retching noise which was interpreted by our hosts as an expression of joy. Several other ladies in the Corps showed a disposition to succumb to the vapours at this piece of intelligence. But the old training dies hard. There was many a tight lip and beady eye but not a word was said until we were assembled for breakfast in the card room of the Slopsy Blob Hotel. Then the pent-up floodwaters of emotion overflowed. Ambassadors, Ministers, Secretaries of Embassy and their wives began as one

19

man to gesticulate and gabble. It was a moving scene. Some called upon the Gods to witness that they would never travel by train again; others spoke wonderingly of the night they had just spent when the whole of their past life flashed before them as if on a screen; the wife of the Spanish Republican Minister, by far the most deeply shaken by events, fell upon the Doyen, the Polish Ambassador, and named him as responsible before God for our safety and well-being. It was an interesting study in national types. The Egyptians screamed, the Finns and Norwegians snarled, the Slav belt pulled at each other's lapels as if they were milking goats. The Greeks made Promethean gestures at everyone. (They could afford to take the Balanced View since they had already hired the only six taxis in Zagreb and were offering seats for the return journey at a thousand dinars each.)

'One thing emerged clearly from all this. The Corps was in a state of open mutiny and would not easily be persuaded to entrain once more with the Brothers Karamazov. The Doyen pleaded in vain. We struck various national attitudes all round the room. The Italian Ambassadress who looked as if her anger would succeed in volatilizing her went so far as to draw up her dress and show the company a bruise inflicted on her during the journey. As for Polk-Mowbray, he did indeed have a scalp wound – an egg-shaped protuberance on the crown of his head where he had doubtless been struck by a passing railway station. It was clear that the journey had aged him.

'Well, that day most of us spent the time in bed with cold compresses and aspirin. In the evening we attended a performance of the Ballet and a Torchlight Tattoo. Liberation Day was at an end. That night the Doyen convened another meeting in the hotel at which he harangued us about diplomatic procedure in general and our obligations to the Service in particular. In vain. We were determined not to travel back on the Ghost Train. He pleaded with us but we were adamant. That evening a flock of telegrams fluttered into the Protocol Department of the Ministry of Foreign Affairs – telegrams pleading sudden illness, pressure of work, unforeseen political developments, migraine, influenza, neuritis or Events Beyond the Writer's Control. At dawn a convoy of taxis set out on the homeward track bearing the shattered remnants of the Corps, unshaven, unhonoured, but still alive, still breathing . . . In a way I was sorry for the Brothers Karamazov and the Liberation-Celebration Machine. God knows, one did not wish them ill. But I must confess I was not surprised to read in the paper a week later that this latest triumph of the Yugoslav Heavy Industry had jumped the points at Slopsy Blob and finished the good work it had begun by carrying away most of the station buildings. No one was hurt. No one ever is in Serbia. Just badly shaken and frightened out of one's wits. It is all, when you come to think of it, part of the Serbian Way of Life . . .'

CASE HISTORY

Last week, Polk-Mowbray's name came up again – we had read of his retirement that morning in *The Times*. We had both served under him in Madrid and Moscow, while Antrobus himself had been on several missions headed by him – Sir Claud Polk-Mowbray, OM, KCMG, and all that sort of thing.

Talking of him, Antrobus did his usual set of facial jerks culminating in an expression like a leaky flowerpot and said: 'You know, old man, thinking of Polk-Mowbray today and all the different places we've served, I suddenly thought "My God, in Polk-Mowbray we have witnessed the gradual destruction of an Ambassador's soul".'

I was startled by this observation.

'I mean', went on Antrobus, 'that gradually, insidiously, the Americans got him.'

'How do you mean, "the Americans got him"?'

Antrobus clicked his tongue and lofted his gaze.

'Perhaps you didn't know, perhaps you were not a Silent Witness as I was.'

'I don't honestly think I was.'

'Do you remember Athens '37, when I was first secretary?'

'Of course.'

'Polk-Mowbray was a perfectly normal well-balanced Englishman then. He had all the fashionable weaknesses of the eighteenth-century gentleman. He fenced, he played the recorder.'

'I remember all that.'

'But something else too. Think back.'

'I'm thinking . . .'

Antrobus leaned forward and said with portentous triumph:

'He wrote good English in those days.' Then he sat back and stared impressively at me down the long bony incline of his nose. He allowed the idea to soak in.

Of course what he meant by good English was the vaguely orotund and ornamental eighteenth-century stuff which was then so much in vogue. A sort of mental copperplate prose.

'I remember now', I said, 'committing the terrible sin of using the phrase "the present set-up" in a draft despatch on economics.' (It came back gashed right through with the scarlet pencil which only Governors and Ambassadors are allowed to wield – and with something nasty written in the margin.)

'Ah,' said Antrobus, 'so you remember that. What did he write?'

' "The thought that members of my staff are beginning to introject American forms into the Mother Tongue has given me great pain. I am ordering Head of Chancery to instruct staff that no despatches to the Foreign Secretary should contain phrases of this nature." '

'Phew.'

'As you say – phew.'

'But Nemesis', said Antrobus, 'was lying in wait for him, old chap. Mind you,' he added in the sort of tone which always sounds massively hypocritical to foreigners simply because it is, 'mind you, I'm not anti-American myself – never was, never will be. And there were some things about the old Foreign Office Prose Style – the early Nicolson type.'

'It was practically Middle English.'

'No, what I objected to was the Latin tag. Polk-Mowbray was always working one in. If possible he liked to slip one in at the beginning of a despatch. *"Hominibus plenum, amicis vacuum* as Cato says," he would kick off. The damnable thing was that at times he would forget whether it was Cato who said it. I was supposed to know, as Head of Chancery. But I never did. My classics have always been fluffy. I used to flash to my Pears Encyclopedia or my Brewer, swearing all the time.'

'He sacked young Pollit for attributing a remark in Tacitus to Suetonius.'

'Yes. It was very alarming. I'm glad those days are over.'

'But Nemesis. What form did he take?'

'She, old man. *She.* Nemesis is always a woman. Polk-Mowbray was sent on a brief mission to the States in the middle of the war.'

'Ah.'

'He saw her leading a parade wrapped in the Stars and Stripes and twirling a baton. Her name was Carrie Potts. She was what is known as a majorette. I know. Don't wince. No, he didn't marry her. But she was a Milestone, old fellow. From then on the change came about, very gradually, very insidiously. I noticed that he dropped the Latin tag in his drafts. Then he began to leave the "u" out of words like "colour" and "valour". Finally, and this is highly significant, he sent out a staff circular saying that any of the secretaries caught using phrases like *quid pro quo, sine qua non, ad hoc, ab initio, ab ovo* and *status quo* would be transferred. This was a bombshell. We were deprived at a blow of practically our whole official vocabulary. Moreover as he read through the circular I distinctly heard him say under his breath: "This will pin their ears back." You can imagine, old fellow, I was stiff with horror. Of course, the poor fellow is not entirely to blame; he was fighting the disease gamely enough. It was just too much for him. I found a novel by Damon Runyon in his desk-drawer one day. I admit that he had the good taste to blush when he saw I'd found it. But by this time he had begun to suffer from dreadful slips of the tongue. At a cocktail party for instance he referred to me as his "sidekick". I was too polite to protest but I must admit it rankled. But there was a much more serious aspect to the business. His despatches began to take a marked transpontine turn. By God, you'll never believe it but I kept coming across expressions Like "set-up", "frame-up", "come-back", and even "gimmick". I ask you – *gimmick.*' Antrobus blew out his breath in a cloud of horror. 'As you can imagine,' he went on after a pause, 'the FO was troubled by the change in his reporting. Worst of all, other Ministers and Ambassadors junior to him and easily influenced showed some disposition to copy this sort of thing. Finally it got to such a pitch that all despatches before being printed in Intel-summary form had to pass through a sieve: they established an office in the Rehabilitation section specially for deformed English. Then you remember the Commission on Official English and the book called *Foreign Office Prose – How to Write It*?'

'Yes. One of the worst-written books I've ever read.'

'Well, be that as it may, it was the direct outcome of Polk-Mowbray's activities. It was a last desperate attempt to stop the rot, old man. It was too late, of course, because by this time that dreadful Churchill chap was wandering all over the globe in a siren suit waving a Juliet at everyone. I need hardly add that Mowbray himself ordered a siren suit which he referred to as his "sneakers". He used to potter round the Embassy grounds in them – a bit furtively, of course, but nevertheless . . . there it was.' Antrobus paused for a long moment as he sorted out these painful memories. Then he said grimly, under his breath, and with dark contempt: 'Faucet, elevator, phoney. I *ask* you.'

'Yes,' I said.

'Hatchet-man . . . disc-jockey . . . torch-singer.'

'Yes. Yes. I follow you.'

'It was terribly sad. Poor Polk-Mowbray. Do you know that he went to a Rotary meeting in a hand-painted tie depicting a nude blonde and referred to it in his speech as "pulchritudinous"?'

'Never.'

'He did.' Antrobus nodded vigorously several times and took a savage swig at his drink. 'He absolutely did.'

'I suppose', I said after a moment, 'that now he is retiring he will settle over there and integrate himself.'

'He was offered a chance to go to Lake Success as a specialist on Global Imponderables, but he turned it down. Said the IQ wasn't high enough – whatever that meant. No, it's even more tragic. He has taken a villa outside Rome and intends to summer in Italy. I saw him last week when I came back from the Athens Conference.'

'You saw him?'

'Yes.' Antrobus fell into a heavy brooding silence, evidently stirred to the quick. 'I don't really know if I should tell you this,' he said in a voice with a suspicion of choking in it. 'It's such a nightmare.'

'I won't repeat it.'

'No. Please don't.'

'I won't.'

He gazed sadly at me as he signed his bar slips, waiting in true Foreign Office style until the servant was out of earshot. Then he leaned forward and said: 'I ran into him near the *Fontana*, sitting in a little *trattoria*. He was dressed in check plus-fours with a green bush jacket and a cap with a peak. He was addressing a plate of spaghetti – and *do you know what*?'

'No. What?'

'There was a *Coca Cola* before him with a straw in it.'

'Great heavens, Antrobus, you are jesting.'

'My solemn oath, old man.'

'It's the end.'

'The very end. Poor Polk-Mowbray. I tried to cringe my way past him but he saw me and called out.' Here Antrobus shuddered. 'He said, quite distinctly, quite unequivocally, without a shadow of doubt – he said: "*Hiya!*" and made a sort of gesture in the air as of someone running his hand listlessly over the buttocks of a chorus girl. I won't imitate it in here, someone might see.'

'I know the gesture you mean.'

'Well,' said Antrobus bitterly, 'now you know the worst. I suppose it's a symptom of the age really.' As we sauntered out of his club, acknowledging the porter's greeting with a nod, he put on his soft black hat and put his umbrella into the crook of his arm. His face had taken on its graven image look – 'a repository of the nation's darkest secrets'. We walked in silence for a while until we reached my bus stop. Then he said: 'Poor Polk-Mowbray. In Coca Cola veritas what?'

'Indeed,' I said. There could not be a better epitaph.

JOTS AND TITTLES

'In Diplomacy,' said Antrobus, 'quite small things can be One's Undoing; things which in themselves may be Purely Inadvertent. The Seasoned Diplomat keeps a sharp eye out for these moments of Doom and does what he can to avert them. Sometimes he succeeds, but sometimes he fails utterly – and then Irreparable Harm ensues.

'Foreigners are apt to be preternaturally touchy in small ways and I remember important negotiations being spoilt sometimes by a slip of the tongue or an imagined slight. I remember an Italian personage, for example (let us call him the Minister for Howls and Smells), who with the temerity of ignorance swarmed up the wrong side of the C-in-C Med's Flagship in Naples harbour with a bunch of violets and a bottle of Strega as a gift from the Civil Servants of Naples. He was not only ordered off in rather stringent fashion but passes were made at him with a brass-shod boathook. This indignity cost us dear and we practically had to resort to massage to set things right.

'Then there was the Finnish Ambassador's wife in Paris who slimmed so rigorously that her stomach took to rumbling quite audibly at receptions. I suppose she was hungry. But no sooner did she walk into a room with a buffet in it than her stomach set up growls of protest. She tried to pass it off by staring hard at other people but it didn't work. Of course, people not in the know simply thought that someone upstairs was moving furniture about. But at private dinner parties this characteristic was impossible to disguise; she would sit rumbling at her guests who in a frenzy of politeness tried to raise their voices above the noise. She soon lost ground in the Corps. Silences would fall at her parties – the one thing that Diplomats fear more than anything else. When silences begin to fall, broken only by the rumblings of a lady's entrails, it is The Beginning of the End.

'But quite the most illuminating example of this sort of thing occurred on the evening when Polk-Mowbray swallowed a moth. I don't think I ever told you about it before. It is the sort of thing one only talks about in the strictest confidence. It was at a dinner party given to the Communist People's Serbian Trade and Timber Guild sometime during Christmas week back in '52. Yugoslavia at that time had just broken with Stalin and was beginning to feel that the West was not entirely populated by "capitalist hyenas" as the press said. They were still wildly suspicious of us, of course, and it was a very hot and embarrassed little group of peasants dressed in dark suits who accepted Polk-Mowbray's invitation to dinner at the Embassy. Most of them spoke only their mother tongue. Comrade Bobok, however, the leader of the delegation, spoke a gnarled embryonic English. He was a huge sweating Bosnian peasant with a bald head. His number two, Pepic, spoke the sort of French that one imagines is learned in mission houses in Polynesia. From a diplomatist's point of view they were Heavy Going.

'I shall say nothing about their messy food habits; Drage the butler kept circling the table and staring at them as if he had gone out of his senses. We were all pretty sweaty and constrained by the time the soup plates were removed. The conversation was early cave-man stuff consisting of growls and snarls and weird flourishes of knife and fork. Bobok and Pepic sat on Polk-Mowbray's right and left respectively; they were flanked by Spalding the Commercial Attaché and myself. We were absolutely determined to make the evening a success. De Mandeville for some curious reason best known to himself had decreed that we should eat turkey with mustard and follow it up with plum pudding. I suppose it was because it was Christmas week. Comrade Bobok fell foul of the mustard almost at once and only quenched himself by lengthy potations which, however, were all to the good as they put him into a good temper.

'The whole thing might have been carried off perfectly well

Comrade Bobok

had it not been for this blasted moth which had been circling the Georgian candlesticks since the start of the dinner-party and which now elected to get burnt and crawl on to Polk-Mowbray's side-plate to die. Polk-Mowbray himself was undergoing the fearful strain of decoding Comrade Bobok's weighty pleasantries which were full of corrupt groups and he let his attention wander for one fatal second.

'As he talked he absently groped in his side-plate for a piece of bread. He rolls bread balls incessantly at dinner, as you know. Spalding and I saw in a flash of horror something happen for which our long diplomatic training had not prepared us. Mind you, I saw a journalist eat a wine-glass once, and once in Prague I saw a Hindu diplomat's wife drain a glass of vodka under the impression that it was water. She let out a moan which still rings in my ears. But never in all my long service have I seen an Ambassador eat a moth – and this is precisely what Polk-Mowbray did. He has a large and serviceable mouth and into it Spalding and I saw the moth disappear. There was a breathless pause during which our poor Ambassador suddenly realized that something was wrong; his whole frame stiffened with a dreadful premonition. His large and expressive eye became round and glassy with horror.

'This incident unluckily coincided with two others; the first was that Drage walked on with a blazing pudding stuck with holly. Our guests were somewhat startled by this apparition, and Comrade Bobok, under the vague impression that the blazing pud must be ushering in a spell of diplomatic toasts, rose to his feet and cried loudly: "To Comrade Tito and the Communist People's Serbian Trade and Timber Guild. *Jiveo!*" His fellow Serbs rose as one man and shouted: "*Jiveo!*"

'By this time, however, light had begun to dawn on Polk-Mowbray. He let out a hoarse jarring cry full of despair and charred moth, stood up, threw up his arms and groped his way to the carafe on the sideboard, shaken by a paroxysm of coughing. Spalding and I rocked, I am sorry to say, with hysterical giggles, followed him to pat him on the back. To the startled eyes of the Yugoslavs we must have presented the picture of three diplomats laughing ourselves to death and

Sir Claud Polk-Mowbray, OM, KCMG

slapping each other on the back at the sideboard, and utterly ignoring the sacred toast. Worse still, before any of us could turn and explain the situation Spalding's elbow connected with Drage's spinal cord. The butler missed his footing and scattered the pudding like an incendiary bomb all over the table and ourselves. The Yugoslav delegation sat there with little odd bits of pudding blazing in their laps or on their waistcoats, utterly incapable of constructive thought. Spalding, I am sorry to say, was racked with guffaws now which were infectious to a degree. De Mandeville who was holding the leg of the table and who had witnessed the tragedy also started to laugh in a shrill feminine register.

'I must say Polk-Mowbray rallied gamely. He took an enormous gulp of wine from the carafe and led us all back to table with apologies and excuses which sounded, I must say, pretty thin. What Communist could believe a capitalist hyena when he says that he has swallowed a moth? Drage was flashing about snuffing out pieces of pudding.

'We made some attempt to save the evening, but in vain. The awful thing was that whenever Spalding caught De Mandeville's eye they both subsided into helpless laughter. The Yugoslavs were in an Irremediable Huff and from then on they shut up like clams, and took their collective leave even before the coffee was served.

'It was quite clear that Spalding's Timber Pact was going to founder in mutual mistrust once more. The whole affair was summed up by the *Central Balkan Herald* in its inimitable style as follows: "We gather that the British Embassy organized a special dinner at which the Niece de Resistance was Glum Pudding and a thoroughly British evening was enjoyed by all." You couldn't say fairer than that, could you?'

FRYING THE FLAG

'Of course, if there had been any justice in the world,' said Antrobus, depressing his cheeks grimly. 'If we ourselves had shown any degree of responsibility, the two old ladies would have been minced, would have been incinerated. Their ashes would have been trampled into some Serbian field or scattered in the sea off some Dalmatian island, like Drool or Snot. Or they would have been sold into slavery to the Bogomils. Or just simply crept up on from behind and murdered at their typewriters. I used to dream about it, old man.'

'Instead of which they got a gong each.'

'Yes. Polk-Mowbray put them up for an MBE. He had a perverted sense of humour. It's the only explanation.'

'And yet time softens so many things. I confess I look back on the old *Central Balkan Herald* with something like nostalgia.'

'Good heavens,' said Antrobus, and blew out his cheeks. We were enjoying a stirrup-cup at his club before taking a turn in the park. Our conversation, turning as it always did upon our common experiences abroad in the Foreign Service, had led us with a sort of ghastly inevitability to the sisters Grope; Bessie and Enid Grope, joint editor-proprietors of the *Central Balkan Herald* (circulation 500). They had spent all their lives in Serbia, for their father had once been Embassy chaplain and on retirement had elected to settle in the dusty Serbian plains. Where, however, they had inherited the old flat-bed press and the stock of battered Victorian faces, I cannot tell, but the fact remains that they had produced between them an extraordinary daily newspaper which remains without parallel in my mind after a comparison with newspapers in more than a dozen countries – 'THE BALKAN HERALD KEEPS THE BRITISH FLAG

33

FRYING' – that was the headline that greeted me on the morning
of my first appearance in the Press Department. It was typical.

The reason for a marked disposition towards misprints was
not far to seek; the composition room, where the paper was
hand-set daily, was staffed by half a dozen hirsute Serbian
peasants with greasy elf-locks and hands like shovels. Bowed
and drooling and uttering weird eldritch-cries from time to time
they went up and down the type-boxes with the air of half-
emancipated baboons hunting for fleas. The master printer was
called Icic (pronounced Itchitch) and he sat forlornly in one
corner living up to his name by scratching himself from time to
time. Owing to such laborious methods of composition the
editors were hardly ever able to call for extra proofs; even as it
was the struggle to get the paper out on the streets was
grandiose to watch. Some time in the early thirties it had come
out a day late and that day had never been made up. With
admirable single-mindedness the sisters decided, so as not to
leave gaps in their files, to keep the date twenty-four hours
behind reality until such times as, by a superhuman effort, they
could produce two newspapers in one day and thus catch up.

Bessie and Enid Grope sat in the editorial room which was
known as the 'den'. They were both tabby in colouring and wore
rusty black. They sat facing one another pecking at two ancient
typewriters which looked as if they had been obtained from the
Science Museum or the Victoria and Albert.

Bessie was News, Leaders, and Gossip; Enid was Features,
Make-up and general Sub. Whenever they were at a loss for copy
they would mercilessly pillage ancient copies of *Punch* or *Home
Chat*. An occasional hole in the copy was filled with a ghoulish
smudge – local blockmaking clearly indicated that somewhere a
poker-work fanatic had gone quietly out of his mind. In this way
the *Central Balkan Herald* was made up every morning and then
delivered to the composition room where the chaingang rapidly
reduced it to gibberish. MINISTER FINED FOR KISSING IN PUBIC.
WEDDING BULLS RING OUT FOR PRINCESS. QUEEN OF HOLLAND GIVES
PANTY FOR EX-SERVICE MEN. MORE DOGS HAVE BABIES THIS SUMMER
IN BELGRADE. BRITAINS NEW FLYING-GOAT.

In the thirties this did not matter so much but with the war and the growth of interest in propaganda both the Foreign Office and the British Council felt that an English newspaper was worth keeping alive in the Balkans if only to keep the flag flying. A modest subsidy and a free news service went a long way to help the sisters, though of course there was nothing to be done with the crew down in the composition room. 'Mrs Schwartkopf has cast off clothes of every description and invites inspection.' 'In a last desperate spurt the Cambridge crew, urged on by their pox, overtook Oxford.'

Every morning I could hear the whistles and groans and sighs as each of the secretaries unfolded his copy and addressed himself to his morning torture. On the floor above, Polk-Mowbray kept drawing his breath sharply at every misprint like someone who has run a splinter into his finger. At this time the editorial staff was increased by the addition of Mr Tope, an elderly catarrhal man who made up the news page, thus leaving Bessie free to follow her bent in paragraphs on gardening ('How to Plant Wild Bubs') and other extravagances. It was understood that at some time in the remotest past Mr Tope had been in love with Bessie but he 'had never Spoken'; perhaps he had fallen in love with both sisters simultaneously and had been unable to decide which to marry. At all events he sat in the 'den' busy with the world news; every morning he called on me for advice. 'We want the *Herald* to play its full part in the war effort,' he never failed to assure me gravely. 'We are all in this together.' There was little I could do for him.

At times I could not help feeling that the *Herald* was more trouble than it was worth. References, for example, to 'Hitler's nauseating inversion – the rocket-bomb' brought an immediate visit of protest from Herr Schpünk, the German *chargé*, dictionary in hand, while the early stages of the war were greeted with BRITAIN DROPS BIGGEST EVER BOOB ON BERLIN. This caused mild speculation as to whom this personage might be. Attempts, moreover, to provide serious and authoritative articles for the *Herald* written by members of the Embassy shared the same fate. Spalding, the commercial attaché who was trying to negotiate on behalf of the British Mining Industry, wrote a painstaking survey of the wood resources of Serbia which appeared under the startling banner BRITAIN TO BUY SERBIAN TIT-PROPS, while the military attaché who was rash enough to contribute a short strategic survey of Suez found that the phrase 'Canal Zone' was printed without a 'C' throughout. There was nothing one could do. 'One feels so desperately ashamed,' said Polk-Mowbray, 'with all the resources of culture and so on that we have – that a British newspaper abroad should put out such disgusting gibberish. After all, it's semi-official, the Council has subsidized it specially to spread the British Way of Life. . . . It's not good enough.'

But there was nothing much we could do. The *Herald* lurched from one extravagance to the next. Finally in the columns of Theatre Gossip there occurred a series of what Antrobus called Utter Disasters. The reader may be left to imagine what the Serbian compositors would be capable of doing to a witty urbane and deeply considered review of the 100,000th performance of *Charley's Aunt*.

The *Herald* expired with the invasion of Yugoslavia and the sisters were evacuated to Egypt where they performed prodigies of valour in nursing refugees. With the return to Belgrade, however, they found a suspicious Communist régime in power which ignored all their requests for permission to refloat the *Herald*. They brought their sorrows to the Embassy, where Polk-Mowbray received them with a stagey but absent-minded sympathy. He agreed to plead with Tito, but of course he never did. 'If they start that paper up again,' he told his Chancery darkly, 'I shall resign.' 'They'd make a laughing stork out of you, sir,' said Spalding. (The pre-war mission had been returned almost unchanged.)

Mr Tope also returned and to everyone's surprise had Spoken and had been accepted by Bessie; he was now comparatively affluent and was holding the post which in the old days used to be known as Neuter's Correspondent – aptly or not who can say?

'Well, I think the issue was very well compounded by getting the old girls an MBE each for distinguished services to the British Way of Life. I'll never forget the investiture with Bessie and Enid in tears and Mr Tope swallowing like a toad. And all the headlines Spalding wrote for some future issue of the *Herald*: "Sister Roasted in Punk Champagne after solemn investiture".'

'It's all very well to laugh,' said Antrobus severely, 'but a whole generation of Serbs have had their English gouged and mauled by the *Herald*. Believe me, old man, only yesterday I had a letter from young Babic, you remember him?'

'Of course.'

'For him England is peppered with fantastic place names which he can only have got from the *Herald*. He says he enjoyed visiting Henleg Regatta and Wetminster Abbey; furthermore, he was present at the drooping of the colour; he further adds that the noise of Big Bun striking filled him with emotion; and that he saw a film about Florence Nightingale called "The Lade With the Lump". No, no, old man, say what you will the *Herald* has much to answer for. It is due to sinister influences like the Gropes and Topes of this world that the British Council's struggle is such an uphill one. Care for another?'

FOR IMMEDIATE RELEASE

'Most FO types', said Antrobus, 'are rather apt to imagine that their own special department is more difficult to run than any other; but I must say that I have always handed the palm to you Information boys. It seems to me that Press work has a higher Horror Potential than any other sort.'

He is right, of course. Antrobus is always right, and even though I am no longer a foreign service type I am proud to be awarded even this tardy recognition when all is said and done.

A press officer is like a man pegged out on an African ant-hill for the termites of the daily press to eat into at will. Nor are we ever decorated. You never read of a press officer getting the George Cross for rescuing a reporter who has fallen into his beer. Mostly we just sit around and look as if we were sickening for an OBE.

And what can compare with the task of making journalists feel that they are loved and wanted – without which they founder in the Oedipus Complex and start calling for a Parliamentary Commission to examine the Information Services? Say what you like, it's an unenviable job.

Most of the press officers I've known have gradually gone off their heads. I'm thinking of Davis who was found gibbering on the Nan Tal Pagoda in Bangkok. All he could say was: 'For Immediate Release, absolutely immediate release.' Then there was Perry who used to boil eggs over a spirit-lamp in the office. He ended by giving a press conference in his pyjamas.

But I think the nicest and perhaps the briefest press officer I have ever known was Edgar Albert Ponting. He was quite unique. One wonders how he was recruited into so select a cadre. He was sent to me as second secretary in Belgrade. I had been pressing for help for some time with a task quite beyond

38

me. The press corps numbered some fifty souls – if journalists can be said to have souls. I could not make them all feel loved and wanted at once. Trieste with its ghastly possibilities of a shooting war loomed over us: propaganda alone, I was told, could keep the balance – could keep it a shouting war. I turned to the Foreign Office for help. Help came, with all the traditional speed and efficiency. After two months my eleventh telegram struck a sympathetic chord somewhere and I received the information that Edgar Albert was on the way. It was a great relief. Fraternization with the press corps had by this time raised my alcohol consumption to thirty *slivovitza* a day. People said they could see a pulse beating on the top of my head. My Ambassador had taken to looking at me in a queer speculative way, with his head on one side. It was touch and go. But it was splendid to know that help was at hand. It is only forty odd hours from London to Belgrade. Ponting would soon be at my elbow, mechanically raising and lowering his own with the old Fleet Street rhythm press officers learn so easily.

Mentally, I toasted Ponting in a glass of sparkling Alka Seltzer and called for the *Immediate* file. From Paris came the news that he had not been found on the train. After a wait of four days a signal came through saying that he had been found. He was at present in St Anne's due for release later in the day when his journey would be resumed. I was rather uneasy as I remembered that St Anne's was a mental hospital, but my fears subsided as I followed his route and saw him safely flagged into Switzerland and down into Italy. There was an ominous pause at Pisa which lasted ten days. Then came a signal from the Embassy in Rome saying that our vice-consul there had located him and put him on the train. This was followed by an odd sort of telegram from Ponting himself which said: *'Can't tell you what impression Leaning Tower made on me old man. On my way. Avanti. Ponty.'*

At Venice there was another hold-up, but it was brief. Our vice-consul was away. It appeared that Ponting had borrowed 1,000 lire from the consulate gondolier and represented himself to the clerks in the consulate as a distressed British subject domiciled in Lisbon. All this was of course disquieting, but, as I say, one gets used to a highly developed sense of theatre in press

39

officers. They live such drab lives. Once he was through Trieste and Zagreb, however, I began to breathe more freely, and make arrangements to meet him myself.

The Orient Express gets in at night. I had planned a quiet little dinner at the flat during which I would unburden myself to Ponting and brief him as to the difficulties which faced us. (A visit from the Foreign Minister impended: rumours of Russian troop movements were at meridian: trade negotiations with Britain were at a delicate phase: and so on and so forth.)

He was not at the station: my heart sank. But Babic, the Embassy chauffeur, interrogated the wagon-lit attendant, and we learned with relief that Ponting had indeed arrived. 'He must have walked,' said the attendant, 'he had very little luggage besides the banjo. A little case like a lady's handbag.'

We drove thoughtfully up the ill-paved streets of the capital and down Knez Mihailova to the only hotel set aside for foreign visitors (all the others had been turned into soup-kitchens and communal eating-houses). He was not at the hotel. I was standing at the desk, deep in thought, when the circular swing-doors of the hotel began to revolve, at first with slowness, then with an ever-increasing velocity which drew the eyes of the staff towards them. Somebody not too certain of his bearings was trying to get into the hotel. It seemed to me that he was rather over-playing his hand. By now the doors were going round so fast that one thought they would gradually zoom up through the ceiling, drawn by centrifugal force. Ponting was inside, trapped like a fly in amber. I caught sight of his pale self-deprecating face as he rotated grimly. It was set in an expression of forlorn desperation. How had this all come about? Could he have mistaken these massive mahogany doors for a bead curtain? Impossible to say. He was still holding his banjo to his bosom as he swept round and round. There was an impressive humming noise as of a nuclear reactor reacting, or of a giant top at full spin. Ponting looked dazed but determined, like a spinster trapped in a wind-tunnel. A small crowd of servants formed at a respectful distance to observe this phenomenon. Then without warning the second secretary was catapulted out of the swing-doors into our midst, like someone being fired out of a gun into a net. We

Edgar Albert Ponting

recoiled with him, falling all over the staircase. For a brief moment his face expressed all the terror of a paralytic whose wheelchair has run away with him and is heading straight for the canal. Then he relaxed and allowed himself to be dusted down, gazing anxiously at his banjo all the time. 'Thank God, Ponting, at last you're here,' I said. I don't know why I should take the name of God in vain at a time like this; the words just slipped out.

He introduced himself in rather a mincing fashion. His eyes were certainly glassy. I put him down as a rather introverted type. I must say, however, that his opening remark 'could not but' (as we say in despatches) fill me with misgiving. 'This "*slivovitza*",' he said hoarsely, 'it's a damn powerful thing. I'm practically clairvoyant, old man. You mustn't be shirty with old Ponting.' He wagged a finger forlornly, helplessly. He looked as if he too needed to feel loved and wanted.

Physically he was on the small side, pigeon-chested and with longish arms which ended in fingers stained bright yellow with nicotine. He had the mournful innocent eyes of a mongrel. 'Ponting,' I said, 'you'd better have a little rest before dinner.' He did not protest, but leaning heavily against me in the lift he said under his breath, but with conviction: 'If ever I get the Nobel Prize it won't be for nuclear physics.' In my heart of hearts I could not help agreeing with him.

He laid himself out on his bed, kicked off his shoes, folded his arms behind his head, closed his eyes and said (in the veritable accents of Charlie McCarthy): 'Quack. Quack. Quack. This is Ponting calling.' Then in a different voice: 'Did you say Ponting? Surely not Ponting.' Then reverting again to the dummy he so much resembled: 'Yes, Ponting. *The* Ponting, Ponting of Ponte-fract.'

'Ponting,' I said severely.

'Quack Quack,' responded the dummy.

'Ponting, I'm going,' I said.

He opened his eyes and stared wildly round him for a moment. 'Is it true that the Ambassador lives on nightingale sandwiches?' he asked. There were tears in his eyes. 'The *Daily Express* says so.' I gave him a glance of cold dignity.

'I shall speak to you tomorrow,' I said, 'when you are sober.' I meant it to sting.

By eleven o'clock next morning Ponting had not appeared and I sent the office car for him. He was looking vague and rather scared and had a large woollen muffler round his throat. His eyes looked as if they were on the point of dissolving, like coloured sweets. 'Old man,' he said hoarsely, 'was there something you wanted?'

'I wanted to take you to H.E., but I can't take you looking like an old-clothes-man.' He gazed down at himself in wonder. 'What's wrong with me?' he said. 'I bet you haven't got a shirt on under that scarf.' I had already caught a glimpse of a pyjama jacket. 'Well, anyway,' said Ponting, 'I can sign the book, can't I?'

I led him shambling through the Chancery to the Residence which I knew would be deserted at this hour. He made one or two hypnotist's passes at the Visitors' Book with streaming pen and finally delivered himself of a blob the size of a lemon. 'It was the altitude,' he explained. 'My pen exploded in my pocket.' I was busy mopping the ink with my handkerchief. 'But you came by train,' I said, with considerable exasperation, 'not by air.' Ponting nodded. 'I mean the altitude of the Leaning Tower of Pisa,' he said severely.

I led him back to the Chancery door. 'Can I go back?' he asked humbly. 'It takes a few days to acclimatize in a new post; H.E. won't be shirty with old Ponting, will he?'

'Go,' I said, pointing a finger at the iron gates of the Embassy, 'and don't come back until you are ready to do your job properly.'

'Don't be shirty, old boy,' he said reproachfully. 'Ponting will see you through.'

'Go,' I said.

'In my last post', said Ponting in a brooding hollow sort of way, 'they said I was afflicted with dumb insolence.'

He traipsed down the drive to the waiting car, shaking his head sadly.

I was contorted with a hideous sense of desolation. What was to be done with a ventriloquist who played the banjo and spent half his time talking like a duck?

I went into the Chancery and took down the FO List to examine Ponting's background. His foreground had become only too apparent by now. He had had a number of posts, none of which he had held for more than a month or so; he had been moved round the world at breakneck speed, presumably leaving behind him in each town the indelible scars of a conduct which could only be excused by reference to the severest form of personality disorder. 'Bitter fruit,' I said to Potts the archivist. 'Look at this character's record.' He put on his spectacles and took the book from me. 'Yes,' he said. 'In every post it would seem to be a case of retired hit-wicket. Poor Ponting!'

'Poor Ponting!' I said angrily. 'Poor me!'

After that I did not see Ponting for several weeks. Once, late at night, my Head of Chancery surprised him in the lounge of his hotel doing a soft shoe routine and playing the banjo to a deeply attentive audience of partly sentient journalists. The heavy smell of plum brandy was in the air. In those days it cost about fourpence a glass. Ponting did a little song, a pitiful little spastic shuffle, and brought the performance to an end by pulling out his bow tie to the distance of a yard before letting it slap back on to his dicky. Antrobus, then first secretary, witnessed all this with speechless wonder. 'By God,' he said fervently, 'never have I seen an Embassy let down like this. He popped his cheek at me in a dashed familiar fashion and said he had once acted in a pierrot troupe on Clacton pier. I couldn't bring him to his senses. He was . . .' words failed him. He reported the matter to H.E. who, from the armoury of his diplomatic experience, produced the word which had eluded Antrobus. 'Bizarre,' he said gravely. 'I gather this fellow Ponting is a little bizarre.'

'Yes, sir,' I said.

'It's awfully peculiar,' he said. 'Your predecessor was an Oxford Grouper. He was bizarre too. At press conferences he would jump up and testify to the most awful sins. Finally the press protested.' He paused. 'If you don't mind my saying so,' he said, 'a large proportion of the Information Section in the FO seems a bit . . . well, bizarre.' I could see that he was wondering rather anxiously what my particular form of mental trouble might be.

'I'm afraid Ponting will have to go.'

'Well, if you say so. But as he's been civil enough to sign the book I must give him a meal before he leaves.'

'It would be unwise, sir.'

'Nevertheless I will, poor fellow. You never know what he has on his mind.'

'Very good, sir.'

From then on Ponting became a sort of legendary figure. I tried to find him from time to time but he never seemed to be in. Once he phoned me to say that he was taking up a lot of contacts he had made and that I was not to worry about him. He had made a hit with the press, he added, everybody loved old Ponting and wanted him. I was so speechless with annoyance I forgot to tell him that telegrams suggesting his recall had already been sent to the Foreign Office. One day Antrobus came to my office; he appeared to be within an ace of having a severe internal haemorrhage. 'This man Ponting', he exploded, 'must be got out of the country. Britain's good name . . .' He became absolutely incoherent.

'What's he done now?' I asked. Antrobus for once was not very articulate. He had met Ponting, dressed as a Roman centurion, walking down the main street of the town at twelve noon that morning. He had been, it seemed, to a fancy dress ball given by the Yugoslav ballet and was on his way back to his hotel. 'He was reeling,' said Antrobus, 'absolutely reeling and speechless. Rubber lips, you know. Couldn't articulate. And the bastard popped his cheek at me again. And gave me a wink. Such a wink.' He shuddered at the memory. 'And that's not all,' said Antrobus, his voice becoming shriller. 'That's by no means all. He rang Eliot at three o'clock in the morning and said that H.E. didn't understand the Trieste problem and that he, Ponting, was going to open unilateral negotiations with Tito in his own name. I gather he was prevented by the tommy gunners on Tito's front door from actually carrying out his threat. Mark me, we shall hear more of this.' Ponting's future never looked darker. That afternoon we got a call from the Ministry of Foreign Affairs. They wished to deliver an *aide mémoire* to the Embassy. Montacute went. He was the new Counsellor. He came back an hour later mopping his brow. 'They say Ponting is a Secret Service agent. Unless we withdraw him he'll be declared *persona non grata*.' I gave a sigh of relief. 'Good. This will force the FO's hand. I'll get off an Immediate.' I did. The answer came back loud and clear that evening: *'Edgar Albert Ponting posted to Helsinki to leave by earliest available means.'*

Armed with this telegram I set out to find him. He was not at the hotel, not at the only two restaurants available for foreigners. He was not at the Press Club though Garrick of the *Mirror*, who was expiating his sense of frustration in triple *slivovitzas*, told me he'd seen him. 'He was trapped in the lift some hours ago. Dunno where he went afterwards.' I finally ran him to earth in a Balkan *bistro* with an unpronounceable name. He was sitting at the bar with a girl on each side. His face was lifted to the ceiling and he was singing in a small bronchial voice:

> I'm the last one left on the corner,
> There wasn't a girl for me,
> The one I loved married anovver,
> Yes anovver, yes anovver,
> Oo took 'er far over the sea.

He was so moved by his own performance that he began to cry now, huge round almost solid tears which rained down and marked the dusty bar. This sort of behaviour is fairly normal among Serbs whenever they are drunk and the tragedy of The Great Panslav idea comes to mind. The girls patted him sympathetically on the back. 'Poor old Ponty,' said Ponting in hollow self-commiserating tones. 'Nobody understands Ponty. Never felt loved and wanted.' He blew his nose insanely in a dirty handkerchief and drained his glass. This cheered him. He said in a good strong cockney voice:

> Come fill me with the old familiar jewce
> Mefinks I shall feel better bye and bye . . .

'Ponting,' I said. 'There's some news for you.'

He took the telegram in shaking fingers and read it out slowly like a peasant reading the Creed. 'What's it mean?' he said.

'You're off tomorrow. There's a crisis in Helsinki which brooks of no delay. Ponting, the FO have chosen *you*. Your country is calling.'

'Ta ra ra ra,' he said irreverently and stood to the salute. We were all irresistibly impelled to do the same, the Serbian girls, the bartender and myself. It was the last memory I was to carry away of Ponting. I have often thought of him, and always with affection and respect. Some years ago I saw that he had transferred to the Colonial Office, and from that day forward, believe it or not, you could hardly open a newspaper without reading about a crisis in the colony where Ponting happened to be posted. Maybe it's only the sheer momentum of Ponting's influence which is pushing the Empire downhill at such a speed. I shouldn't be at all surprised.

THE GAME'S THE THING

As for Sport (said Antrobus), the very word makes me uneasy.
I've never believed in its healing power. Once I was forced to
referee a match between HMS Threadbare and the French Fleet
which resulted in my nearly being dismembered. Luckily the
Gents in the pavilion had a bolt and padlock on it or I wouldn't
be here today. No. I regard Sport with Grave Reserve.

Polk-Mowbray was not of my opinion; he believed in the
stuff. Thereby hangs my tale. It was during one of those long
unaccountable huffs between ourselves and the Italians. You
know the obscure vendettas which break out between Missions? Often they linger on long after the people who threw the
first knife have been posted away. I have no idea how this huff
arose. I simply inherited it from bygone dips whose bones were
now dust. It was in full swing when I arrived – everyone
applying freezing-mixture to the Italians and getting the Retort
Direct in exchange. When you saw an Italian at a party you
gave a slow smile amputated by scorn. Yes, we made it clear
that we were pretty miffed about something. They also acted in
a markedly miffed manner. Yet I doubt if anyone on either side
could have explained why we were all so dashed miffed. So
while bows were still exchanged for protocol reasons they were
only, so to speak, from above the waist. A mere contortion of
the dickey, if you take me, as a tribute to manners. A slight
Inclination accompanied by a *moue*. Savage work, old lad,
savage work!

One day, however, the wind changed. Polk-Mowbray called a
senior conference. 'We must end this huff,' he said regretfully.
'Though it goes against the grain. London says that these
dastards are going to vote against us at UNO. We must put aside

our private pleasures and do everything to soothe and mollify the dogs. Our duty calls on us to surrender Our All.' Several ideas for promoting the peace were put up, and at last – O fatal Dovebasket! – there came one which fired Polk-Mowbray's imagination. 'That's it!' he cried. 'Brilliant! Magistral! Prescient! Dovebasket, I salute you! You will go far.'

The idea was this: to challenge the Italian Mission to a football match and lose it gracefully, thus making them feel happy and well-disposed. Now everyone knew that the Italian Chancery was staffed by three guards who had been professionals once – footballers of international pointlessness. The team was a formidable one. To this we would oppose a scratch team of dead-beat dips who would be run off their feet in a quarter of an hour, thus losing by two hundred goals to nothing. Like all Dovebasket's schemes it seemed sound on the face of it, almost ingenious. I had an obscure premonition of doom but I brushed it aside. What could go wrong with such an idea? I did not of course know (none of us did) that two of our own Chancery Guards, Morgan and Bolster, were also internationals and had played for Wales. Furthermore I did not know that Dovebasket was short of money. True he was always hanging about the Chancery sucking the silver head of a swagger-stick and saying: 'I'm fearfully pushed for lolly these days.' I paid no attention, being somewhat pushed myself. Afterwards it all became clear. Dovebasket and De Mandeville were in league. No sooner was the match declared on than they began taking bets *against* instead of *for* the Italians.

Innocently we pushed on with our preparations for this senseless frolic unaware of the trap they were setting for us. Polk-Mowbray spent quite a lot of money from the Secret Service Vote to buy us blue shorts with a polka-dot design and singlets of red, white and blue. I don't suppose we made much of a showing as we bowled on to the field to the polite hand-claps of the Ladies of the Corps. Most of us had that dreadful rinsed-out look which comes from Conferences. We had all constructed heavy shin pads from the Master-Files. I had nearly a week's economic despatches down each stocking. Of course with all this defensive equipment we moved like pregnant water buffaloes.

Without grace, without poetry. But we tried to look as if we meant business.

I must say the three Italian forwards filled me with the liveliest anxiety. They were very large indeed and I noticed that they had long-handled knives in their stockings. I was rather glad that we were all set to lose. The two Ambassadors elected to goal-keep because Heads of Mission don't like to be seen hurrying. All were at last assembled. The pitch was ankle deep in mud and within a moment the ball resembled a half-mixed cake so that even Arturo, Benjamino and Luigi had some difficulty in pushing it about. It was even harder for us. After a few minutes of desultory running about we were all pretty winded and dispersed while the Italians executed some dashing figures of eight all round us, steadily moving down upon the anxious Polk-Mowbray – remorseless as an enema, old man.

Our defence was of the open-work variety and within a very few minutes they had scored a goal. Then another. Then another. Everyone beamed and resisted an impulse to cheer. We embraced them. They embraced us. Polk-Mowbray insisted on planting a fraternal kiss upon the Italian Ambassador's cheek. He, poor man, was deeply moved and clearly no longer miffed in the least. You can say what you like but we British know how to lose gamely. Prefer it, in fact. We had all taken on that frightfully decent look as we puffed about, showing ourselves plucky but inept – in fact in character. Our ladies cheered shrilly and waved their umbrellas.

By half-time we were seven goals down. Singularly few mishaps had occurred. True the Naval Attaché on the wing (who believed in reincarnation) was badly hacked by a free-thinking third secretary, but nobody gave a fig about that. We were losing, that was the main thing. It was not until half-time that Dovebasket's dastardly plan came into action. He and De Mandeville gracefully circulated the refreshments – rum cocktails and acid drops – before announcing their intention of retiring from the game 'to give the replacements a chance'. Both, it seemed, had slipped a disc. Polk-Mowbray was sympathetic, suspected nothing. 'What bad luck,' he cried. And as the whistle went I saw the military attaché's jeep approaching among the

trees with the replacements in it. Two huge figures – Morgan
and Bolster – sat in the back, armed *cap à pie* for the fray. 'Well,
well, Chancery Guards,' cried Polk-Mowbray democratically.
'What an awfully good show! That will freshen us up.' Little did
he know . . .

They were huge, old man. I'd never seen them undressed
before, so to speak. Such thews. Knotted and gnarled. Real
Henry Moore jobs both. And covered in tattooing as well – ships
and crowns and girl-friends' phone numbers. Worst of all they
both wore an air of surly magnificence that can only come from
long leisurely potions of Navy Issue rum. They gave off waves of
jaunty and illicit self-confidence. My heart began to sink as I
watched these case-hardened male-nurses come trotting across
the bog to take their place in our forward line. My blood froze as
I heard Morgan whisper hoarsely: 'Now remember we've got to
do them proper or Dovie won't give us our cut, see?' So that was
it! A cry broke from my lips. It was drowned by the whistle. We
were off like men struggling for life in an ocean of glue.

What a titanic battle now began between the opposing
forwards! The collisions in mid-air, the feints, the sorties, the
trapeze acts! Our innocent little game of push-ball suddenly took
on a starker aspect; it was becoming more like a medieval
butchery in a tilt-yard. The compatriots of Toscanini sent up
musical cries of amazement at this sudden passionate flowering
of a skill they did not guess we owned. By a brilliant system of
double-entry Morgan and Bolster shot four goals in just over five
minutes. Polk-Mowbray began to look faintly alarmed. The
Italians, recovering from their surprise, buckled down to the job.
The barges, the elbowing, the rabbit-punches on the referee's
blind side began to increase. It was clear that we were losing our
amateur status at last. Morgan and Bolster were used to this. For
them it was just like winding in a capstan. Counter-barges and
counter-shoves followed with the occasional dull thwack of a
rabbit-punch. Cries of, 'Foul' and, 'You keek me, yes?' Two
more goals to our credit. 'By thunder!' cried Polk-Mowbray
passionately. 'What is going on?' Well might he ask. Bolster and
Morgan were now playing with the concentrated fury of
religious fanatics who had glimpsed the Promised Land. I don't

know how much money was at stake. The Italians too had begun to get pretty rough. The pace had also increased. Clash followed upon clash. 'Great Heavens!' cried Polk-Mowbray feebly. 'Have they not been briefed, the Guards?' Yes, they had; but alas, not in the intended sense.

There was ten minutes to go when Bolster equalized. A groan went up from Italians and British alike. The Italian Ambassador burst into tears. Arturo began to finger the knife in his stocking and mutter. I felt quite faint just looking at him. The whistle again. By now everyone seemed to have become infected by pure rage. I received a kick from De Ponzo (ordinarily the mildest of men, a father, a bird-watcher) – a kick which left traces. I'll show you some time. In fact from a diplomatic football match the thing was steadily becoming a spectacle of unbridled bestiality. Such pushing, such cuffing, such heaving and bumping I have never witnessed before or since. And the language – a Saturnalia of Swearing, old man. If I hadn't been so scared I would have blushed to the roots of my CMG. Then at last it came – the dire *coup de grâce*.

Bolster opened fire with a boom like a sixteen-inch gun right from the popping-crease as it were. There was cold and dire malevolence about the shot. The sodden leather fairly winged through the sky towards the uncorseted form of the Italian Chief of Mission. Mind you, for an ethereal sort of man he was quite spirited and did not flinch. There was a hollow concussion followed by a yell as our distinguished colleague received the charge full in the midriff. I felt things going black all round me. What a shot! Yes, and what a casualty – for the poor Ambassador, propelled backwards through his own goal by the sheer force of this flying pudding, was soon lying senseless in the ditch. It seemed to me that all they could do now was to draw a mackintosh reverently over the body before resuming play – as they do at Twickenham. *We were now leading by one goal.* Imagine our despair! Polk-Mowbray was dancing with rage and consternation in our goal mouth. The Ladies were screaming shrilly. Drage was holding a mirror to the Italian Ambassador's lips and shaking his head sadly. On all sides rose cries for help. Messengers began running in all directions for ambulances.

And it was now that the tactless Bolster cried merrily:
'Another eight minutes to go.' And this tore it, to use a vulgar
phrase, tore it good and proper right down the centre. The
Italian forwards closed in on him with the manifest intention of
wiping the smile from his lips. Morgan intervened. Blows began
to be exchanged. The Naval Attaché was struck down. Other
peacemakers tried unwisely to intervene. The referee was
gouged and swallowed the pea in his whistle. A scuffle now
started destined to end in a riot. Knives were drawn. There were
slashes and screams. The ladies shrieked in unison. It was nearly
ten minutes before the Vulgarian Flying-Squad arrived and
surged on to the pitch armed with tommy-guns. We were all
under arrest. We were ignominiously handcuffed together for
nearly an hour before the *doyen* could persuade them that we
were privileged dips and not subject to the civil penalties of riot.
Those not on the list – our forwards and theirs – were carried
away in a plain van. The whole thing ended in a scandal.

And our neat little plan? What is there to add? The vote went
against us at UNO, and the Italians stayed miffed. To add insult
to injury Dovebasket's Christmas Card that year showed a
Father Xmas in football-boots. Yes, of course they stayed miffed.
I bet you the miff remains unrequited to this day.

No, you'll never catch me joking about sport.

WHITE MAN'S MILK

'The Grape,' said Antrobus with a magisterial air as he stared into the yellow heart of his Tio Pepe, 'the Grape is a Rum Thing. I should say it was the Diplomat's Cross – just as I should say that in diplomacy a steady hand is an indispensable prerequisite to doing a job well . . . Eh? The tragedies I've seen, old boy; you'd never credit them.'

'Ponting?'

'Well, yes – but I wasn't even thinking of the element of Human Weakness. But just think of the varieties of alcoholic experience which are presented to one in the Foreign Service. To take one single example – National Days.'

'My God, yes.'

'To drink vodka with Russians, champagne with the French, *slivovitz* with Serbs, *saki* with Japs, whisky and Coca Cola with the Yanks . . . the list seems endless. I've seen many an Iron Constitution founder under the strain. Some get pooped by one drink more than another. There was a Vice-Consul called Pelmet in Riga . . .'

'Horace Pelmet?'

'Yes.'

'But he didn't drink much, did he?'

'No. But there was one drink which he couldn't take at all. Schnapps. Unluckily he was posted to Riga and then Oslo. At first he was all right. He used to get slightly dappled, that was all. Then he started to get progressively pooped. Finally he became downright marinated. Always crashing his car or trying to climb the sentries outside the Embassy. We managed to hush things up as best we could and he might have held out until he got a transfer to a wine-growing post. But what finished him was a ghastly habit of ending every sentence with a shout whenever he was three or four schnapps down wind. You'd be at a perfectly serious reception exchanging Views with Colleagues when all of a sudden he'd start. You'd hear him say – he started quite low in the scale – "As far as I, Pelmet, am concerned" – and then suddenly ending in a bellow: "British policy IS A BLOODY CONUNDRUM." I heard him do this fourteen times in one evening. The German Minister protested. Of course, poor Pelmet had to go. They held him *en disponibilité* for a year or so but no Chief of Mission would touch him. He died of a broken heart I believe. Took to wood-alcohol on a big scale. Poor fellow! Poor fellow!'

He sighed, drained his glass and raised a long finger in the direction of the bar for reinforcements. Merlin the steward replenished the glasses silently and withdrew.

'But the unluckiest chap of all', continued Antrobus after a short pause, 'was undoubtedly Kawaguchi, the Jap Minister in Prague. His downfall was Quite Unforeseen. Poor chap.'

'Tell me about him.'

'His was a mission of some delicacy. He started off frightfully well. Indeed, they were an enchanting couple, the Kawaguchis. They spoke nothing but Jap, of course, which sounds like someone sand-papering a cheese-wire. With the rest of the Corps they were silent. Both were tiny and pretty as squirrels. Their features looked as if they had been painted on to papier mâché with a fine brush. At functions they sat together, side by side, holding on to their own wrists and saying nothing. But they were full of the small conventional diplomatic politeness – always sending round presents of sweets or paper fans with "Made in Hong Kong" printed on them. Once I saw her laugh – she made a funny clicking sound. As for him, I don't honestly know how he conducted his business with the Czechs. There was some sort of trade pact being discussed at the time. Perhaps he used telepathy. Or perhaps he'd discovered some sort of Central European tic-tac. His whole mission consisted of two typist-clerks and a butler, none of whom spoke Czech. Anyway the important thing is this: the Kawaguchis never drank anything but *saki* which they imported in little white stone

. . . the Kawaguchis . . . were tiny and pretty as squirrels . . .

The speed had increased to something like the Farnborough Air Show.

bottles. As you know it's a sort of brew from millet or something . . .'

'Salty and mildly emetic.'

'Yes: well, when they had to go out to a banquet or rout he always sent his butler over in the afternoon with a few small bottles of the stuff which were always placed before him at table. It was a familiar sight to see the two of them sitting there with their *saki* bottles before them. And so it was on this fatal evening which I am about to describe to you. It was New Year's Eve, I think: yes, and the French had elected to give a party. They always did things better than anyone else. The Kawaguchis were there, sitting in a corner, looking about them with their usual air of dazed benevolence. It was late and the party was in full swing. The usual petty scandals had enjoyed their usual public manifestation – the wife of the Finnish Consul had gone home in a huff because her husband had disappeared into the garden with the wife of the French First Secretary. A Russian diplomat was being sick in the Gentlemen's cloakroom. A nameless military attaché was behaving foully . . . we won't go into that. The general nostalgia had afflicted the band and a whole set of Old Viennese Waltzes was being played non-stop. As you know, it is a jolly difficult dance and can verge on the lethal. I always take cover when I hear "The Blue Danube" coming up, old man.'

'So do I.'

'Well, imagine my astonishment when I saw the Kawaguchis rise from their chairs. They had never been known to dance, and at first I thought they were leaving. But something curious in their attitude drew my attention. They were gazing at the dancers like leopards. They both looked dazed and concentrated – as if they had been attending an ether party. Then he suddenly seized her round the waist and they began to dance, to the astonishment and delight of everyone. And they danced perfectly – a real Viennese waltz, old man, impeccable. I felt like cheering.

'They went round the floor once and then twice: everything under control. Then, old man, a ghastly premonition of the worst came over me, I can't tell why. Was it an optical illusion or were they dancing a bar or two faster than the music? I waited in an agony of impatience for them to come round again. It was only too true. They were one bar, two bars out of time. But their spin was absolute perfection still. By now, of course, the band began to feel the squeeze and increased the time. Indeed, the whole thing speeded up. But as fast as they overtook the Kawaguchis the faster did the two little Japs revolve. Perhaps in some weird Outer Mongolian way they thought it was all a race. I don't know. But I, who know the dangers and pitfalls of the Old Viennese Waltz, felt my throat contract with sympathy for them. There was no way one could help. A terrible blackness of soul came over me – for all his Czech colleagues were there on the floor dancing with their wives. It could only be a matter of time now . . . The speed had increased to something like the Farnborough Air Show. Lots of people had dropped out but the floor was still quite full. The Kawaguchis were still travelling a dozen light-years ahead of the band, and the band with popping eyes was pumping and throbbing at its instruments in an attempt to catch them up. But by now they were no longer a dancing couple. They were a Lethal Weapon.'

Antrobus paused and lit a cigarette with a shaking hand. Then he went on sadly. 'The first to go was the Czech Minister of Finance, with whom Kawaguchi had been doing so frightfully well in negotiation. There was a sudden sharp crack and the next moment he was sitting on a violinist's knee holding his ankle while his wife stood ineffectually beating the air for a moment before subsiding on top of him. The Kawaguchis noticed nothing. They were in a trance. On they went. A series of collisions, trifling in themselves, now began to take place. The Chief Economic Adviser to the Treasury, Comrade Cicic, was dancing with a wife whose massive proportions and enormous buffer constituted a dance floor hazard at the best of times. In a waltz it was hair-raising to image what might happen.

'I calculated that if the Kawaguchis struck her they would certainly be halted dead. Not a bit of it. This frail little couple had achieved such a terrific momentum that when they struck Mrs Cicic there was a dull crash only: a powder-compact in her evening bag exploded causing a cloud of apparent smoke to rise. When it cleared Mrs and Mr Cicic were reeling into the corner while the Kawaguchis were speeding triumphantly on their way. They had entered into the spirit of the waltz so deeply now that they were dancing with their eyes closed. There was something Inscrutably Oriental about the whole thing. I don't remember ever being so excited in my life. I began to tick off the casualties on my fingers. By now there were quite a number of walking-wounded and one or two near-stretcher cases; everywhere one could hear the astonished whispers of the Corps: "C'est Kawaguchi qui l'a fait . . ." "Das ist Kawaguchi . . ." But on they went, scattering destruction, and perhaps they would be going on still had not someone deflected them.

'I still don't quite remember how. All I remember is that all of a sudden they were off the floor and moving through the tables and chairs with the remorselessness of a snow-plough. At the end of the ballroom there were some tall french windows which were open. They opened on to a long terrace at the end of which there was an ornamental lake in the most tasteless post-Versailles tradition. Nevertheless. The Kawaguchis vanished through the french windows like a meteor, and such was the dramatic effect they had created that everyone rushed out after them just to see what would happen, including the band which was somehow still playing. It was just as if someone at a children's party had shouted: "Come and look at the fireworks." We all poured out on the terrace shouting and gesticulating. The Spanish Ambassador was shouting: "For God's sake stop them. STOP THEM. Caramba!" But there wasn't any stopping them.

'The tragic but unbelievably beautiful momentum of their waltz had carried them into the shallow lake. Normally it would be snowbound but Prague had had a thaw this year. They sat, utterly exhausted but somehow triumphant in a foot of water and stench, smiling up at their colleagues of the Corps. The cold night air and the water which enveloped them seemed to be having a calming effect, but they made no effort to get out of the pond. They just stared and smiled quaintly. It was only then that I realized they were both drunk, old man. Absolutely pooped. People had come with lights now, and Czech doctors and alienists had appeared from everywhere. There were even some members of the Czech Red Cross with blankets and stretchers.

'We waded into the swamp to recover our colleague and his wife and after a bit of argument emptied them both into stretchers. I shall never forget her smile of sheer beatitude. Kawaguchi's face expressed only a Great Peace. As they bore him off I heard him say, more to himself than anyone: "Oriental man different from White Man." I have always remembered and treasured that remark, old boy. Something like the same thing was said by the French chargé's wife: "How your Keepling say: 'Ist is Ist and Vest is Vest'?" But I was sorry for the Kawaguchis. Magnificent as the whole thing was, here we were, with three minutes to go before midnight, simply covered in mud and confusion. Some of the women had tried to draw attention to themselves by rushing into the swamp after them. The Italian Ambassador had a sort of Plimsoll line in the middle of his dress trousers. The ballroom looked like an advance dressing-station on the Somme. It is impossible to pretend that the evening wasn't ruined. And above all, the dreadful smell. Apparently all the drains flowed into this romantic little lake. It was all very well so long as it wasn't disturbed. The French were definitely confused, and I for one was sorry for them. No Mission could carry off a thing like this lightly.'

Antrobus blew out his cheeks and lay back in his armchair, keeping a watchful eye on me to see that I had fully appreciated all the points in the drama. Then he went on in his usual churchwarden's style: 'The Kawaguchis left for Tokyo by air the next afternoon. His mission was a failure and he knew it. I must say that there were only two Colleagues at the airport to see him off – myself and the perfectly foul military attaché about whom I will never be persuaded to speak. He was deeply moved that we had troubled to find out the time of his departure from the Protocol. I wrung his hand. I knew he wasn't to blame for the whole thing. I knew it was purely Inadvertent.'

'How do you mean?'

'The butler gave the whole thing away some weeks later. Apparently the normal case of *saki* had not come in that month. They were out of drink. There was nothing a responsible butler of any nationality could do. He took some of the *saki* bottles and filled them with . . . guess what?'

61

'Bad Scotch whisky.'

'Dead right! "White Man's Milk" he called it.'

'Awfully bad luck.'

'Of course. But we face these hazards in the Foreign Service, don't we?'

'Of course we do.'

'And we outlive them. Kawaguchi is in Washington.'

'Bravo! I'm so glad.'

'Care for another whiff of Grape-Shot before we lunch?'

IF GARLIC BE THE FOOD OF LOVE . . .

Every Wednesday now, in the winter, I lunch with Antrobus at his club, picking him up at the Foreign Office just before noon. I think he enjoys these meetings as much as I do for they enable him to reminisce about old times in the Foreign Service. For my part I am always glad to add an anecdote or two to my private *Antrobus File* – the groundwork upon which I one day hope to raise the monument of my own Diplomatic Memories . . .

Yesterday his memory carried him back to Vulgaria again where he had served under Polk-Mowbray – and over De Mandeville – as Head of Chancery. 'Bitter days,' he mused. 'And perhaps one shouldn't talk about them. De Mandeville was in a queer state all that spring; perhaps it had something to do with the phases of the moon? I don't know. He was in a "Hamlet, Revenge!" sort of mood. The trouble seemed to centre about the Embassy table – as Third Sec. he had a watching brief on the food. It started I remembered with a series of Constance Spry table decorations which made that otherwise fairly festive board look like an illustration from the Jungle Books. One could hardly carry a fork to one's mouth without biting off a piece of fern by mistake. Slices of decorative pumpkin and marrow gave a Harvest Festival note to things. One peered at one's guests through a forest of potted plants. Finally Polk-Mowbray put his foot down. De Mandeville became huffed. The next thing was he ordered Drage to serve everything from the right – in deference to a left-handed Trade Mission chief who was staying with us. It may have been tactful but it led to endless complications with us right-handed trenchermen who found everything upside down, and had to scuffle to rearrange our table-patterns as we sat down. And then what with Drage coming in so fast from the wrong side one was practically always out, hit-wicket on the *soufflé*. I tried to reason with De Mandeville but he only pouted and bridled. It was clear that he was in an ugly mood, old boy. I feared the worst. I have a sort of intuition about these things.

'The next thing in this chain of progressive sabotage was curry. De Mandeville had a series of Madras curries served. They were of such a blistering intensity that the entire Dutch Embassy had the inside of its collective mouth burned away – peeled off like bark from a tree, old boy. The Minister called on Polk-Mowbray in *tenue* and wanted to know if a state of war existed between England and Holland. His wife had to be treated for soft palate. A junior attaché went about saying that the Embassy food was full of quicklime and hinting darkly about damages. Naturally there were high words and massive contempts flying about which made Polk-Mowbray somewhat nervy. De Mandeville was sharply taken to task, but without avail. He next served an onion soup and black bread without soup-spoons. You know how long a rich onion soup takes to cool. Our little lunch-party dragged on almost to dusk, and several guests were lightly scalded because they neglected to take thermometer readings before gulping. The whole thing was gradually working up towards a climax. I saw it all coming and mentally, so to speak, closed my eyes and breathed a prayer to the Goddess of Diplomacy. I could not, however, guess from which quarter this warped and twisted Third Sec. might deliver the knock-out blow.

'Then . . . all this is in the strictest confidence, old man . . . Then it came. Polk-Mowbray used to leave his office-door wide open so I could see and hear all that went on therein. One morning I heard a familiar sort of row going on and I knew that the blow had fallen at last. Polk-Mowbray was hysterical. "I adjure you by the bones of Cromer," he was yelling, "to answer me without prevarication. *Have you been putting garlic in the food without telling anyone? Did you*, wittingly or unwittingly plug that *cassoulet*, impregnate that lustreless salad, order the peas to be lightly simmered in the stuff before serving? Answer me at once, or in Heaven's Name I'll – "

'De Mandeville made a gobbling self-deprecating sort of sound and spread his manicured hands as he muttered something about garlic being eaten in all the best London houses. It toned up the nervous system. Some said it was the only specific for scabies. One would have to be very retrograde to imagine . . . And so on in this style. Veins were throbbing all over poor Polk-Mowbray by this time. "Do not try to justify yourself," he thundered. "Answer me with a simple yea or nay. And take that beastly sensual smile off your face. If you choose to dine on heads of raw garlic with your scabrous chauffeur it is your business. But the Embassy table is sacred, do you hear? *Sacred*. If you do not answer truthfully I shall make you the subject of a General Paper to the Foreign Secretary." There was a short silence during which they glared at each other. Then De Mandeville threw back his chin and uttered the word "yes" rather defiantly; he was wearing an obstinate Canine Defence League expression on his face. Polk-Mowbray levitated briefly and banged his desk with a triumphant. "Aha! So you *did*." It was clear that De Mandeville was in for one of those Searching Reproofs. His Chief now began to walk up and down his own carpet as he always did when he was moved. He Pointed The Finger Of Scorn at De Mandeville in no uncertain fashion. "Wretch!" he cried in a shaking voice. "Could you not see the harm that might come from such reckless and criminal cookery? Moreover you choose the *one* lunch party of the year which is of policy importance in order to do me the greatest damage. Think of the Naval Attaché! What has he ever done to merit that unspeakable lunch – at which he ate far too heartily? And my niece Angela – what of her? And the Head of the Foreign Ministry – what of him?"

'De Mandeville tried to make a few unavailing protests. "Enough!" cried Polk-Mowbray hoarsely. "Surely you know that to feed a Naval Attaché garlic is like stoking a coke furnace with dead rats? Did you see his face as he lurched out into the afternoon? You did not know, I suppose, that he was due to lecture to the Sea Wolves on Temperance and Self-Denial at sea? He created a very poor impression in a very short time. The wretch now fears court-martial. He says that now whenever his pinnace is sighted they raise a Yellow Fever flag and forbid him access to the ship. I do not doubt that the dirk-point will be facing him when he walks into the ward-room. All this is on your head and more. Don't interrupt me. That is not all. Do you realize that when I helped the Minister into his car he was making a noise like a bunsen burner? *You* would not care that he had to address the High Praesidium that afternoon on Foreign Affairs – moreover in a language so full of aspirates as to make the gravest demands on his audience! No, *you* would not care, with your pumpkins and pottery and left-handed table arrangements! On you go in your headlong career, weaving these devilish plots around my table. And apart from all this what about *me*. *You* cannot be expected to know that I was booked to read the Lesson at a Memorial Service in the British Baptist Chapel which is notoriously cramped and ill-ventilated. How do you think I felt when I saw the first two rows of the congregation swaying like ripened wheat in an east wind? How do you think I felt when it came to my turn to embrace the hapless widow? She was breathing as if she had slipped her fan-belt. Answer me! You see, you haven't a word to say. You are mumchance as you jolly well ought to be. Fie on you, Aubrey de Mandeville! *You* did not stop to think what effect Angela might have on Cosgrave after such a lunch. The engagement was pretty tremulous as it was – but you snookered the wretched girl well and truly. And what of the typists' pool? Girls keeling over one after another as they tried to take dictation from us. What of them?" For a moment words failed him. His face worked. Then he said in a low murderous tone, from between clenched teeth. "I tell you that from now on there is to be no more garlic. Sage, yes. Thyme, yes. Rosemary, marjoram, dill, cumin, yes. Emphatically yes. But *garlic*, no!" And so the edict went forth and the sale of peppermints in the Naafi dropped off again.'

Antrobus sighed sadly over these memories as he replenished our glasses. Then he said musingly: 'I should say really that Garlic was the biggest Single Cross a Diplomat had to bear in the rough old times. It *had* to be banned, old man. Yet in a sense we were all Living A Lie, like the Americans under Prohibition; for we all secretly yearned after the stuff. (I say this in the strictest confidence. I would not wish to be quoted.) Yet it is strange that this noxious bulb should have such an allure for men. As for diplomats, it played havoc with Confidential Exchanges; and as for dancing with your Ambassadress . . . well. It was the quickest way to get posted. That is why I was so relieved when the Age Of Science dawned. I used to be *against* Science once, and for the Humanities – I freely admit it. But when at last chlorophyl came in I was instantly won over. What a boon and a blessing to dips! What an over-riding sense of relief! Many a breach was healed that day between man and man. Even Polk-Mowbray in the end allowed the salad-bowl to be lightly rubbed with a couple of heads before serving. And I don't know whether you noticed the rather respectable little *ragoût* we have just been eating? Not bad for the Club, is it? But fear nothing! In my pocket lies a phial full of those little grey tablets which make human intercourse a rational, easy, unbuttoned sort of thing again. No more shrinking from pursed lips in The Office. We can hold our heads high once more! Let's drink a final little toast to the Goddess of the FO shall we? I give you Chlorophyl!'

'Did I ever tell you about the time when Drage, the Embassy butler, began to suffer from visions? No? Well, it was dashed awkward for all concerned and Polk-Mowbray was almost forced to Take Steps at the end.

'You probably remember Drage quite well: a strange, craggy Welsh Baptist with long curving arms as hairy as a Black Widow. A moody sort of chap. He had a strange way of gnashing his dentures when he spoke on religious matters until flecks of foam appeared at the corners of his mouth. For many years he had been a fairly devout fellow and always took a prominent part in things like servants' prayers. He also played the harmonium by ear at the English church – a performance to be carefully avoided on Sundays. For the rest one always found him hunched over a penny Bible in the buttery when he should have been cleaning the M of W silver. His lips moved and he made a deep purring sound in his throat as he read. We were all, frankly, rather scared of Drage.

'The awful thing about him was that he wore a wig so obvious that he gave one the impression of having just stepped off the stage after a successful performance as Caliban. It was an indeterminate badger-grey affair which left a startling pink line across his forehead. The gum-like colour of the integument simply didn't match the rocky bluish skin of his face. Everyone knew it was a wig. Nobody ever dared to say so or allude to it.

'As for the visions, he confessed later that they had been gaining on him for some considerable time, and if he never mentioned them before it was because he felt that once we all recognized him as the Lord's Anointed we might give him the sack, or at least ask him to step down in favour of Bertram the

Drage

footman. As you see, there were flashes of reason in the man. But all this intense Bible-squeezing could not help but have an effect on him, and one night at a party given for the Dutch Ambassador he dropped his tray and pointed with shaking finger at the wall behind Polk-Mowbray's head, crying in the parched voice of an early desert father: "Here they come, sor, in all their glory! Just behind you, sor, Elijah up, as sure as I'm standing here!" He then covered his eyes as if blinded by the vision and fell mumbling to his knees.

'While in one sense one felt privileged to be present at Drage's Ascension into Heaven by fiery chariot, nevertheless his timing seemed inconsiderate. First of all poor Polk-Mowbray sprang to his feet and overturned his chair. Our guests were startled. Then to make things worse the Naval Attaché who dabbled in the occult and who hated to be left out of anything pretended to share Drage's vision. I think he had been drinking pink gins. He pointed his finger and echoed the butler. "There they go!" he said in cavernous tones. "Behind you!"

' "What the deuce is it?" said Polk-Mowbray nervously, seating himself once more, but gingerly.

'Benbow slowly moved his pointing finger as he traced the course of the Heavenly Host round the dining-room table. "So clear I can actually touch them", he said. He was now pointing at De Mandeville who had changed colour. He leaned forward and touched the Third Secretary's ear-lobe. De Mandeville gave a squeak.

'As you can imagine the whole atmosphere of our dinner party was subtly strained after this. Bertram led Drage off into the wings in a rather jumbled state and bathed his brow from a champagne bucket. Benbow was sent to Coventry by common consent. Nevertheless, he spent the rest of the evening in high good humour, occasionally pointing his finger and saying indistinctly: "Here they come again." He kept the Dutch looking over their shoulders.

'Naturally, one could not tolerate visions during meals and when Drage recovered Polk-Mowbray told him to cut it out or leave. The poor butler was deeply troubled. Apparently he had discovered that he had never been baptized and this was preying on his mind. "Well," said Polk-Mowbray, "if you think baptism will cure you of visions I can easily arrange with Bishop Toft to give you a sprinkle. He arrives next week."

'Twice a year the Bishop of Malta came in for a couple of days to marry, baptize or excommunicate the members of the Embassy living in exile amidst the pagan Yugoslavs. He was, as you remember, a genial and worldly bishop, but hopelessly absent-minded. He brought in with him a sort of acolyte called Wagstaffe who was spotty and adenoidal and did the washing-up of thuribles or whatever acolytes have to do. He was simply Not There as far as the Things Of This World are concerned. He was a Harrovian. It stuck out a mile. Well, this year the bishop's visit coincided with that of Brigadier Dilke-Parrot. In fact they came in the same car and stood being noisily genial in the hall as their bags were unstrapped. The brigadier, who was large and red and had moustaches like antlers, also came every year on some mysterious mission which enabled him to have two days' shooting on the snipe-marshes outside the town. He always brought what he was pleased to call his "*Bundook*" with him – a twelve-bore by Purdy. This year there appeared to be two gun-cases – pay attention to this – and the second one belonged to the bishop. It contained a magnificent episcopal crook, taller when all the bits were screwed together than the bishop himself. These two very similar cases lay side by side in the hall. Thereby hangs my tale.

'Drage greeted Bishop Toft with loud cries of delight and weird moppings and mowings and tugs at his forelock. He explained his case and the bishop rather thoughtfully agreed to baptize him. But here there was an unexpected hitch: Drage refused to be baptized in his wig; he wanted to feel the Jordan actually flowing on his cranium, so it was agreed that the baptism should take place in the privacy of the buttery where the butler could reveal all. A drill was worked out. After the ceremony Drage would replace his foliage and the bishop would then walk ahead of him, holding his crook, to the ballroom where the rest of the Embassy staff would be waiting to receive his ministrations. There were half a dozen babies to baptize that year.

'Well, Drage knelt down, and there was a tearing noise like old canvas. A large polished expanse of dome was presented to the bishop. He said afterwards that he blenched rather because Drage looked so extraordinary. Bits of dry glue were sticking to his scalp here and there. Well, the Bishop of Malta was just about to read the good news and anoint the butler when Wagstaffe opened the leather case and found that it contained the brigadier's "*bundook*". It was imperative to acquaint the bishop with this mishap as he could hardly walk into the crowded Embassy ballroom holding a shotgun like a hillbilly. But how to interrupt Toft who by now was in mid-peroration? Wagstaffe had always been an irresolute person. He could hardly call out: "Hey, look at this for an episcopal crook." He fitted the barrel and stock together with the vague idea of holding it up for the bishop to see. He did not look to see if it was loaded. He started working his way stealthily round the kneeling Drage to where he might catch the bishop's eye.

'But it was the eye of the butler which first lighted on the weapon. He had always been a suspicious person and now it seemed as clear as daylight that while the bishop was holding him in thrall Wagstaffe had orders to stalk him from behind and murder him. Perhaps the shot would be a signal for the massacre of Baptists everywhere. Drage's Welsh heritage came to the surface multiplying his suspicions. And to think that this silver-haired old cleric went about getting Baptists murdered . . . A hoarse cry escaped his lips.

'The irresolute acolyte started guiltily, and as Drage scrambled to his feet, he dropped the gun on to the carpet where it went off. The brigadier had always boasted of its hair-trigger action.

'The dull boom in the buttery sounded frightfully loud to the rest of us in the ballroom across the corridor. It was followed by a spell of inarticulate shouting and then all of a sudden Drage appeared, running backwards fairly fast, pursued by the bishop with his sprinkler, making vaguely reassuring gestures and noises. Wagstaffe staggered to the door deathly pale and fainted across the two front rows of as yet unbaptized babes. They set up a dreadful concert of frightened screams.

'It was a dreadful scene as you can imagine. Drage disappeared into the garden and was only persuaded to come back and finish his baptism by the united efforts of Benbow, De Mandeville and myself. Moreover, he felt humiliated to be seen wigless by the whole Embassy. It took some time to straighten things out, specially as the mud-stained brigadier had by now arrived in a fearful temper, holding the episcopal crook between finger and thumb with an expression of the deepest distaste on his face.

'But as it happens things turned out very well. A pair of bright brown eyes had observed the downfall of Drage. To Smilija, the second housemaid, Drage's baldness seemed a wonderful thing. She had never realized how beautiful he could be until she saw his cranium taking the sunlight. It was a revelation and love now entered where formerly indifference only was . . . They are married now; the visions have stopped; his wig has been sold as a prop to the Opera Company. You occasionally see it in the chorus of *Parsifal*. Which illustrates another little contention of mine: namely that Everybody Is Somebody's Cup Of Tea. Another one before we dine?'

WHERE THE BEE SUCKS . . .

One is at a loss (said Antrobus) when one looks back on those
rough old times to account for the thin but rich vein of fatuity
which ran through the character of Polk-Mowbray. Though in
many ways an admirable Chief of Mission, a talented and self-
disciplined man, nevertheless, he was in others simply a babe in
arms, old boy, a babe in arms.

The main thing I think was that he was subject to Sudden
Urges. He was over-imaginative, he was highly strung. One
week for example it would be Sailors' Knots. It was all right so
long as he only sat at his desk playing with string but this was
not all. He grew reckless, ambitious, carried away by all this new
knowledge. He took to demonstrating his powers at children's
parties, charity bazaars, cocktails – everywhere. And the awful
thing was that his tricks never worked. He trussed the German
Ambassador's eldest son up so tightly that the child nearly
suffocated; we just released him in time with the help of the
garden shears. Drage had to pour a pail of sweet iced Cup all
over the little swollen Teuton face to revive the brat. Then Polk-
Mowbray tied himself to the Embassy door-knob and could not
disengage. Quite a crowd gathered. It was humiliating. Once
more we had to resort to the shears. I took to keeping a pair of
them handy in my office. As Head of Chancery you can imagine
how my responsibilities weighed upon me . . .

'Antrobus,' he used to say to me as he sat abstractedly making
love-knots in a length of high quality manila. 'Antrobus, I am in
the wrong profession. Only just realized it. I should have been
sent to sea as a youth. Round the Cape in a sou'wester, what?
That should have been my life, Antrobus.' Who was I, as his
junior, to contradict?

Two days later I came in to find his typist spliced to the Chancery radiator by one swollen wrist. She was in tears. Polk-Mowbray could not release her and nor could I. 'Tut tut,' he kept saying. 'And such a simple little running bowline too. It is most vexing. I was just trying to show Angela a wrinkle or two.' In the end, Morgan the Chancery guard was forced to pull the radiator out of the wall to free her. Water poured out into De Mandeville's office and ruined a Persian carpet he prized. Obviously things had gone far enough. We had a secret meeting and delegated to Butch Benbow, the Naval Attaché, the task of crushing this little hobby before the whole Corps was infected by it. We knew that in his present mood Polk-Mowbray reverenced all seafaring men – even if they were martyrs to sea-sickness as Butch Benbow was . . . I must say, though, he was clever, was Butch. But then you can always count on the Navy. He asked Polk-Mowbray outright whether he wasn't *afraid* to go on playing with string at such a rate – and on such a scale?

'Afraid?' said the Chief of Mission mildly. 'Why afraid?'

'The last Ambassador to suffer from stringomania', said Butch earnestly, 'hung himself.' He went *krik krik* with his mouth and drew a string round his neck with his finger. Then, to complete the pantomime he rolled his eyes up into his skull until only the whites showed and stuck out a large – and I must say somewhat discoloured and contused – tongue. 'He's quite right, sir,' I said. Polk-Mowbray looked from one to the other, quite startled. 'But sailors do it all the time,' he said.

'Sailors can untie themselves when they wish,' said Butch somewhat stiffly. 'Besides they don't walk in their sleep like you do, sir. The Ambassador I spoke of was also a sleep-walker.' This really made Polk-Mowbray jump. It was one of those lucky hits. Actually he had only once walked in his sleep – though the result was disastrous. I'll tell you about it sometime. It was after a prawn curry devised by De Mandeville. He sat staring at us for a long time with popping eye. Then he sighed regretfully and we knew that for him the days of sail were numbered.

'Thank you for your solicitude,' he said.

Well, that was only an example: I really wanted to tell you about the infernal bees. One day I walked into his office and found him clad for the most part in a beekeeper's veil and gauntlets and holding a sort of tuning-fork with which, as I understand it, you pick up the Queen. I was aghast, but he only waved airily and told me to sit down. 'Antrobus,' he said, 'I have the answer to the monotony of this post. The murmur of innumerable bees, dear boy. A *pastoral* hobby, suitable for diplomats. Something that harms no one, and which yields honey for tea.' All around him lay magazines and brochures entitled *Profitable Bee Keeping*, *The Hornet and Bee Guide*, *The Bee-Fancier* – and that sort of thing. It was clear that he had been delving deeply into bee lore. 'I have ordered a hive from Guernsey', he said, 'and asked the Bag Room to send them on.' 'The Bag Room,' I faltered. 'But surely livestock is on the proscribed list?' The people who make up the Diplomatic Bag as you know are pretty touchy and there are endless rules and regulations about what you can and can't send by bag. Polk-Mowbray shook his head. 'I've looked up the regulations,' he said, 'there is nothing about bees. The chief prohibition is on liquids, but a hive of bees isn't liquid.' I doubted the soundness of his reasoning. Liquids were proscribed because once in the old days a young attaché had sent a bottle of inferior Chianti back to his mother and it had exploded. Most of Lord Cromer's despatches had to be hung out to dry before serving, and some of them actually turned green. The bottle must have been sinfully corked. But then Italian wine . . . Anyway, I still didn't like to think of the Bag Room trustingly accepting a cardboard box with a few holes in the top. 'What if they make honey among the confidential despatches?' I said. He laughed airily. 'Pouf!' he said. 'There will be no difficulty about that. You will see.'

I said no more. Seven days later a disgraceful scene took place on the platform at Venice. The bees, maddened by their solitude in the bag, broke out and stormed into the first-class carriage where Fothergill the courier was eating a ham sandwich. They stung him. He, poor fellow, was attached by a padlock to the sack and could not free himself in time. The next thing was the spectacle of the FO's senior courier running howling across the town waving a bag out of which poured bees and confidential reports in ever increasing quantities. The other couriers, in a vain attempt to help followed him in a sort of demonic paper-chase which only ended at St Marks, where Fothergill took sanctuary behind the altar. Here the darkness foxed the bees and they turned their attention to the priests. And our mail? Old man, it was all at the bottom of the Grand Canal. The consul general was forced to set out with a fleet of gondolas to rescue it before it fell into Unauthorized Hands. You can imagine what a scandal. Fothergill arrived beeless and bagless and under a threat of Excommunication. I thought this would cure Polk-Mowbray. Not a bit. The next lot were sent out by air in an airtight container and Drage was sent to meet them at the airport. A hive had been rigged up in the garage and Polk-Mowbray walked about the Residence in his veil waiting for his blasted bees with feverish professional impatience. At last the moment came. He knew just how to tip them out, and so on. But the bees took violent exception to the hive and within a matter of seconds were darkening the sky. They flew round and round in a desultory fashion at first and then with a roar flew into a drainpipe and emerged in the Chancery where they settled in the old tin stove by the bookcase. For a while everyone was on guard but the little creatures were quite well behaved. 'Live and let live,' cried Polk-Mowbray sucking his thumb. (He had been stung.) 'If the brutes want to live here we shall respect their wishes.' I thought it a bit hard on the junior secretaries but what could I say?

But somewhat to my surprise the bees gave no trouble whatsoever; indeed as time went on their subdued murmuring helped rather than hindered the composition of despatches. Polk-Mowbray rather lost interest in them: from time to time he would put on his veil and peer up the stove-pipe, calling upon them to be good boys and come out for a fly round, but much to everyone's relief they ignored him. Gradually nobody thought of them at all. But alas! This was not to be the end of the story. When the bees finally did emerge they created unparalleled havoc. It was all due to a new secretary, Sidney Trampelvis, who had been insufficiently briefed, and who, on a whim, filled the stove with old betting slips he no longer needed and blithely set them alight. Now at this time there was one of those Ineffably

Delicate Conferences taking place in the committee-room, presided over by no less a personage than Lord Valerian – you know, the Treasury chap. It was all about a trade pact – I must not reveal the details. Now this fellow Valerian – rather a bounder I thought – for some reason awed Polk-Mowbray. I don't know why. Perhaps he had highly placed relations in the FO. Perhaps it was his enormous beard which hung down like a fire curtain and only parted occasionlly when he moved to reveal a strip of OE tie. Typical of course. The rumour was that he used to wear his OE tie in bed, over his pyjama jacket. Well, we Wykehamists can only raise lofty eyebrow over this sort of gossip – which by the way we never repeat. Well, there we all were in solemn conclave when there arose a confused shouting from the Chancery where Trampelvis was receiving the first thrust, so to speak. There followed a moment of silence during which Valerian cleared his throat and was about to launch himself again, and then there came a tremendous hum followed by the sound of running feet. I did not know Drage was capable of such a turn of speed. Into the room he bounded – perhaps with some vague idea of saving his Chief, perhaps of issuing a general gale warning. But it was too late. They were upon us in a compact and lethal cloud, flying very low and with stings at the ready. The confusion was indescribable. Have you ever seen *bees* on a fighter sweep, old boy? Ever felt them crawling up your trousers, down your collar, into your waistcoat? One would have to have nerves of steel not to shriek aloud. To judge by the noises we started making it would be clear that diplomatic nerves are made not so much of steel as of raffia. People began beating themselves like old carpets. Polk-Mowbray after one plaintive cry of, 'My bees,' seized a poker and started behaving like Don Quixote with a set of particularly irritating windmills. Drage lapsed into Welsh religious verse punctuated by snarls and a sort of involuntary pole-jumping. I hid myself in the curtains and extinguished the bees as hard as I could. But the awful thing was that the Queen (I imagine it was her) made a bee-line (to coin a metaphor) for the Drury Lane beard of Lord Valerian who as yet had not fully grasped the situation. He looked down with ever-growing horror to find them swarming

78

blithely in it, with the obvious intention of setting up house there. He was too paralysed to move. (I think personally that he used to spray his beard with Eau de Portugal before committee meetings and this must have attracted the Queen.) Mind you this all happened in a flash. Polk-Mowbray, what with guilt and solicitude for Valerian, was almost beside himself; no sacrifice, he felt, was too great to save the day. In a flash of gallantry he seized the garden shears which had been lying on the mantelpiece (pitiful relic of the days when he played with string) and with a manful though ragged snip . . . divested the Chairman of both beard and OE tie at one and the same stroke . . . I cannot say it improved Valerian's temper any more than his appearance – Polk-Mowbray had sliced rather badly. But there it was. Walking wounded had to retire to the buttery for a Witch Hazel compress. The bees, having done their worst, flew out of the window and into the Ministry of Foreign Affairs across the road. I did not wait to see the sequel. I was so grateful for emerging from this business unscathed that I tip-toed back to my office and rang down to the buttery. I don't mind admitting that I ordered a Scotch and Soda, and a stiffer one than usual. I would even admit (under pressure, and *sotto voce*) that you might have seen a faint, fugitive smile graven upon my lips. I was not entirely displeased, old man, with Polk-Mowbray's method of dealing with an OE tie. In my view it was the only one. Was it, I wondered, too much to hope that it might become More General?

'NOBLESSE OBLIGE'

'The case of Aubrey De Mandeville is rather an odd one. I often wonder what the poor fellow is doing now. He wasn't cut out for Diplomacy – indeed it puzzles me to think how Personnel Branch could have considered him in any way the answer to a maiden's prayer at all. It was all due to Polk-Mowbray's folly, really.'

'I don't remember him.'

'It was the year before you came.'

'Polk-Mowbray was Ambassador?'

'Yes. He'd just got his KCMG and was feeling extremely pleased about it. He'd invited his niece Angela to spend the summer at the Embassy and it was I think this factor which preyed on his mind. This Angela was rather a wild young creature – and as you know there was not much to do in Communist Yugoslavia in those days. I think he rather feared that she would fall in with a hard-drinking Serbian set and set the Danube on fire. His dearest wish was that she should marry into the Diplomatic, so he hit upon a brilliant scheme. He would order someone suitable through Personnel and do a bit of match-making. Scott-Peverel the Third Secretary was married. He would have him replaced by Angela's hypothetical Intended. A dangerous game, what? I warned him when I saw the letter. He wanted, he said, a Third Secretary, Eton and Caius, aged 25 (approx), of breeding and some personal fortune, who could play the flute. (At this time he was mad about an Embassy Quartet which met every week to fiddle and scrape in the Residence.) He must have known that you can't always depend on Personnel. However, despite my admonitions he sent the letter off and put the wheels in motion for Bunty Scott-Peverel's

Aubrey De Mandeville

transfer to Tokyo. That was how we got De Mandeville. On paper he seemed to fill the bill adequately, and when his Curriculum Vitae came Polk-Mowbray was rather disposed to crow over me. But I kept my own counsel. I had Doubts, old boy, Grave Doubts.

'They were unshaken even by his personal appearance ten days later, sitting bolt upright in the back of a Phantom Rolls with the De Mandeville arms stencilled on the doors. He was smoking a cheroot and reading the Racing Calendar with close attention. His chauffeur was unloosing a cataract of white pig-skin suitcases, each with a gold monogram on it. It was quite clear that he was a *parvenu*, old boy. Moreover the two contending odours he gave off were ill-matched – namely gin-fumes and violet-scented hair lotion of obviously Italian origin. He condescendingly waved a ringed hand at me as I introduced myself. It had been, he said, a nerve-racking journey. The Yugoslavs had been so rude at the border that poor Dennis had cried and stamped his foot. Dennis was the chauffeur. "Come over, darling, and be introduced to the Man," he cried. The chauffeur was called Dennis Purfitt-Purfitt. You can imagine my feelings, old man. I felt a pang for poor Polk-Mowbray and not less for Angela who was lying upstairs in the Blue Bedroom sleeping off a hangover. "Dennis is my pianist as well as my chauffeur," said De Mandeville as he dismounted holding what looked like a case of duelling pistols but which later turned out to be his gold-chased flute.

'I must confess that I was a bit gravelled for conversational matter with De Mandeville. "I'll take you to meet H.E. at eleven," I said huskily, "if you would like time for a rest and a wash. You will be staying a night or two in the Residence until your flat is ready."

' "Anything you say, darling boy," he responded, obviously determined to be as agreeable as he knew how. In my mind's eye I could see Angela weeping hot salt tears into her pillow after her first meeting with De Mandeville. It was just another of Personnel's stately little miscalculations. However, I held my peace and duly presented him all round. His interview with Polk-Mowbray lasted about fifteen seconds. Then my telephone rang: Polk-Mowbray sounded incoherent. It is clear that he had received a Mortal Blow. "This ghastly fellow," he spluttered. I tried to soothe him. "And above all," said Polk-Mowbray, "impress on him that no Ambassador can tolerate being addressed as 'darling boy' by his Third Secretary." I told De Mandeville this with a good deal of force. He curled his lip sadly and picked his nose. "Now you've hurt little Aubrey," he said reproachfully. "However," and he drew himself together adding: "Little Aubrey mustn't pout." You can imagine, old boy, how I felt.

'De Mandeville's job as Third Secretary was largely social, looking after appointments and visitors and arranging *placements*. I could not help trembling for Polk-Mowbray. The new Third Secretary would sit there at his desk taking snuff out of a gold-chased snuff-box and reading despatches through a huge magnifying glass. He was a *numéro* all right.

'His first act was to paint his flat peacock blue and light it with Chinese lanterns. He and the chauffeur used to sit about in Russian shirts under a sun-lamp playing nap or manicuring their nails. Angela went steadily into a decline. Once when he was an hour late for dinner at the Embassy he excused himself by saying that he had gone upstairs to change his rings and had been simply unable to decide which to wear. He used to have his hair waved and set every month, and made the mistake of going to a Serbian hairdresser to have it done. You know how game the Serbs are, old man? Terribly willing. Will always do their best. They waved De Mandeville's hair into the crispest bunch of curls you are ever likely to see outside Cruft's. It was ghastly. Polk-Mowbray was almost beside himself. He wrote a long offensive letter to Personnel accusing them of sending out a steady stream of female impersonators to foreign posts and smirching the British name, etc.

'De Mandeville himself seemed impervious to criticism. He just pouted. So long as he confined his social activities to his own sphere he was not dangerous. But as time went on he found the diplomatic round rather boring and decided to take the Embassy in hand. His *placements* became more vivid. He also began a series of ill-judged experiments with the Residency Menus.

Some of the more nauseating local edibles found their way on to the Embassy sideboards under stupefying French names. I remember a dinner at which those disgusting Dalmatian sea slugs were served, labelled *"Slugs Japonaises au Gratin"*. The naval attaché went down after this meal with a prolonged nervous gastritis. A Stop Had To Be Put to De Mandeville; of course by now Polk-Mowbray was working night and day to have him replaced – but these things take time.

'Meanwhile the Third Secretary swam in the diplomatic pool in a hair net, took a couple of Siamese kittens for walks with him on a lead, and smoked cigarettes in a holder so long that it was always catching in things.

'His final feat of *placement* – he was dealing with Central European Politburo members of equal rank – was to have the Embassy dining-table cut in half and a half-moon scooped out of each end. When it was fitted together again there was a hole in the middle for H.E. to sit in while his guests sat round the outer circle. Polk-Mowbray was furious. He suffers terribly from claustrophobia and to be hemmed in by this unbroken circle of ape-like faces was almost more than flesh and blood could stand.

'On another occasion De Mandeville dressed all the waiters in Roman togas with laurel wreaths: this was to honour the twenty-first birthday of the Italian Ambassador's daughter. On the stroke of midnight he arranged for a flock of white doves to be released – he had hidden them behind screens. Well, this would have been all right except for one Unforeseen Contingency. The doves flew up as arranged and we were all admiration at the spectacle. But the poor creatures took fright at the lights and the clapping and their stomachs went out of order. They flew dispiritedly round and round the room involuntarily bestowing the Order of the Drain Second Class on us all. You can imagine the scene. It took ages to shoo them through the french windows into the garden. The Roman waiters had to come on with bowls and sponges and remove the rather unorthodox decorations we all appeared to be wearing.

'But the absolute *comble* was when, without warning anyone, he announced that there would be a short cabaret to amuse the Corps at a reception in honour of Sir Claud Huft, the then

Minister of State. The cabaret consisted of De Mandeville and his chauffeur dressed as Snow Maidens. They performed a curious and in some ways rather spirited dance ending in an abandoned *can-can*. It was met with wild applause: but not from Polk-Mowbray as you can imagine. He found the whole episode Distasteful and Unacceptable. De Mandeville left us complete with pigskin suitcases, flute-case, and chauffeur in the Great Rolls. We were all quite dry-eyed at the leave-taking. But it seemed to me then that there was a Moral to be drawn from it all. Never trust Personnel Branch, old man.

'As for poor Angela she was a sad case. Polk-Mowbray sent her to Rome for the Horse Show and – guess what? She up and married a groom. It was a sort of involuntary rebound in a way. Everyone was spellbound with shame. But she had the good sense to go off to Australia with him, where I gather that one needs little Protective Colouring, and there they are to this day. The whole thing, old man, only goes to show that You Can't Be Too Careful.'

CRY WOLF

'The case of Wormwood', said Antrobus gravely, 'is one which deserves thought.'

He spoke in his usual portentous way, but I could see that he was genuinely troubled.

'It is worth reflecting on,' he went on, 'since it illustrates my contention that nobody really knows what anybody else is thinking. Wormwood was cultural attaché in Helsinki, and we were all terrified of him. He was a lean, leathery, saturnine sort of chap with a goatee and he'd written a couple of novels of an obscurity so overwhelming as to give us an awful inferiority complex in the Chancery.

'He never spoke.

'He carried this utter speechlessness to such lengths as to be almost beyond the bounds of decency. The whole Corps quailed before him. One slow stare through those pebble-giglamps of his was enough to quell even the vivid and charming Madame Abreyville who was noted for her cleverness in bringing out the shy. She made the mistake of trying to bring Wormwood out. He stared at her hard. She was covered in confusion and trembled from head to foot. After this defeat, we all used to take cover when we saw him coming.

'One winter just before he was posted to Prague, I ran into him him at a party, and finding myself wedged in behind the piano with no hope of escape, cleared my throat (I had had three Martinis) and said with what I hoped was offensive jocularity: "What does a novelist think about at parties like these?"

'Wormwood stared at me for so long that I began to swallow my Adam's Apple over and over again as I always do when I am out of countenance. I was just about to step out of the window

86

into a flower-bed and come round by the front door when he . . . actually spoke to me: "Do you know what I am doing?" he said in a low hissing tone full of malevolence.

' "No," I said.

' "I am playing a little game in my mind," he said, and his expression was one of utter, murderous grimness. "I am imagining that I am in a sleigh with the whole Diplomatic Corps. We are rushing across the Steppes, pursued by wolves. It is necessary, as they keep gaining on us, to throw a diplomat overboard from time to time in order to let the horses regain their advantage. Who would you throw first . . . and then second . . . and then third. . . ? Just look around you."

'His tone was so alarming, so ferocious and peremptory, that I was startled; more to humour him than anything else, I said "Madame Ventura". She was rather a heavily-built morsel of ambassadress, eminently suitable for wolfish consumption. He curled his lip. "She's gone already," he said in a low, hoarse tone, glowering. "The whole Italian mission has gone – brats included."

'I did not quite know what to say.

' "Er, how about our own Chancery?" I asked nervously.

' "Oh! They've gone long ago," he said with slow contempt, "they've been gobbled up – including you." He gave a yellowish shelf of rat-like teeth a half-second exposure, and then sheathed them again in his beard. I was feeling dashed awkward now, and found myself fingering my nose.

'I was relieved when I heard he had been posted.

'Now, old boy, come a series of strange events. The very next winter in Prague – that was the severe one of '37 when the wolf-packs came down to the suburbs – you may remember that two Chancery Guards and a cipher clerk were eaten by wolves? They were, it seems, out riding in a sleigh with the First Secretary Cultural. When I saw the press reports, something seemed to ring in my brain. Some half-forgotten memory . . . It worried me until I went to the Foreign Office List and looked up the Prague Mission. It was Wormwood. It gave me food for deep thought.

'But time passed, and for nearly ten years I heard no more of Wormwood. Then came that report of wolves eating the Italian

Ambassador on the Trieste-Zagreb road in mid-winter. You remember the case? The victim was in a car this time. I do not have to tell you who was driving. Wormwood.

'Then once again a long period of time passed without any news of him. But yesterday . . .' Antrobus's voice trembled at this point in the narrative and he drew heavily on his cigar.

'Yesterday, I had a long letter from Bunty Scott-Peverel who is Head of Chancery in Moscow. There is a passage in it which I will read to you. Here it is . . .

' "We have just got a new Cultural Sec., rather an odd sort of fellow, a writer I believe. Huge fronded beard, pebble specs and glum as all highbrows are. He has taken a *dumka* about twenty miles outside Moscow where he intends to entertain in some style. Usually these hunting lodges are only open in the summer. But he intends to travel by *droshky* and is busy getting one built big enough, he says, to accommodate the whole Dip. Corps which he will invite to his housewarming. It is rather an original idea, and we are all looking forward to it very much and waiting impatiently for this giant among *droshkies* to be finished."

'You will understand', said Antrobus, 'the thrill of horror with which I read this letter. I have written at length to Bunty, setting out my fears. I hope I shall be in time to avert what might easily become the first wholesale pogrom in the history of diplomacy. I hope he heeds my words. But I am worried, I confess. I scan the papers uneasily every morning. Is that the *Telegraph*, by any chance, protruding from the pocket of your mackintosh?'

CALL OF THE SEA

'I have never really respected Service Attachés,' said Antrobus. 'Some I have known have bordered on the Unspeakable – like that ghastly Trevor Pope-Pope. I don't know how he got into the Blues, nor why he was ever posted to us. He used to lock himself into the cipher-room and play roulette all day with the clerks. Skinned them all, right and left. He had no mercy on anyone. He also used to sell bonded champagne by the case to disagreeable Latin-American Colleagues for pesos. And to cap it all the fellow wore embroidered bedsocks.

'But as for "Butch" Benbow, he was one of the least objectionable service postings. He was naval attaché, you remember.'

'Yes.'

'The fact that he was so decent makes the whole episode inexplicable. I really cannot decide in my own mind whether he did sever that tow-rope or not. And yet I saw him with my own eyes. So did Spalding. Yet the whole thing seems out of keeping with Benbow. But who knows what obscure promptings may stir the heart of a naval attaché condemned to isolation in Belgrade, hundreds of dusty miles from the sound of the sea? And then, imagine being designated to a country with almost no recognizable fleet. There was nothing for him to do once he had counted the two ex-Japanese condemned destroyers and the three tugs which made up Yugoslavia's quota of naval strength. Nor can the horse-drawn barges on the two dirty rivers, the Sava and the Danube, have had much appeal. They filled him no doubt with a deep corroding nostalgia for the open sea and The Men Who Go Down To It In Ships. This might explain the sudden brainstorm which overpowered him when he saw the

entire Diplomatic Corps afloat on the Sava. Human motives are
dark and obscure. I find it hard in my heart to judge Benbow.'

'When was all this?'

'The year after you were posted.'

Antrobus waved his cigar and settled himself more deeply in
his favourite arm-chair. 'It was a slack period diplomatically and
as always happens during slack periods the Corps busied itself
in trying to see which Mission could give the most original
parties. The Americans gave an ill-judged moonlight bathing
party on the island of Spam during which the Corps swam as
one man into a field of jellyfish and a special plane had to be
chartered to bring medical supplies to those who were stung.
Then the Italians, not to be outdone, gave a party in a ruined
monastery surrounded with cherry orchards – a picturesque
enough choice of *venue*. But the season was well advanced and
they had entirely failed to take into account the Greater Panslav
Mosquito – an entomological curiosity to be reckoned with. It is
the only animal I know which can bite effortlessly through
trousers and underpants all in one flowing movement. We all
came back to Belgrade terribly swollen up and all different
shapes and sizes. Then the Finns gave a concert of Serbian folk
music to which the band turned up drunk. Finally it seemed to
Polk-Mowbray that it was our turn to be creative and a chit was
passed down asking for ideas.

'I think it was De Mandeville who suggested a river party.
Certainly it was not Benbow's idea; he had been very subdued
that winter and apart from confessing that he was clairvoyant at
parties and dabbling in astrology he had lived an exemplary life
of restraint.

'Nor, on the face of it, was the idea a bad one. All winter long
the logs come down the River Sava until the frost locks them in;
with the spring thaw the east bank of the river has a pontoon of
tree-trunks some forty feet wide lining the bank under the
willows so that you can walk out over the river, avoiding the
muddy margins, and swim in the deep water. The logs
themselves are lightly tacked together with stapled wire by the
lumberjacks and they stay there till the autumn when they are
untacked again and given a push into mid-stream. They then

'Butch' Benbow

float on down to the sawmills. Here, as you know, the diplomatic corps swims all summer long. Though the muddy banks of the stream are infested with mosquitoes the light river wind ten yards from the shore creates a free zone. And jolly pleasant it is, as you probably remember.

'Well, this was the site selected for a river party by candle-light – the summer nights are breathlessly still – and Polk-Mowbray threw himself into the arrangements with great abandon. First of all he made sure that over the selected area the logs were really tacked firmly together. An immense tarpaulin was then spread and nailed down. This made a raft about a hundred feet by sixty – big enough even to dance on. The Sava water cushioned the thing perfectly. A light marquee was run up and a long series of trestles to take a buffet. It promised to be the most original party of the year – and I'm not sure in retrospect whether it wasn't the most original I have ever attended. De Mandeville and his chauffeur were in the seventh heaven of delight; they organized a wickerwork fence round the raft with little gates leading to the dance floor and so on. There was also a changing-room for those who might decide to stay on and bathe. All in all it was most creditable to those concerned.

'The Corps itself was in ecstasies as it climbed the brightly painted gangplank on to the raft with its gaily lit buffet and striped marquee. Everyone turned up in full splendour and Polk-Mowbray himself made what he called his Special Effort: the cuff-links given to him by King Paul of Greece, the studs given to him by Queen Marie of Rumania, the cigarette-case by De Gaulle, and the cigar-cutter by Churchill. Darkness and candlelight and the buzz of Diplomatic Corps exchanging Views were offset by the soft strains of Bozo's Gypsy Quartet which played sagging Serbian melodies full of glissandos and vibratos and long slimy arpeggios. It was an enchanting scene. The Press Corps was represented by poor Tope (Neuter's Special Corres-pondent) who was rapidly transported into nirvana by the awfully good Bollinger.

'You will ask yourself how the thing could possibly have gone wrong – and I cannot answer you for certain. All I know is that out of the corner of my eye I think I caught sight of a figure – was it Benbow? – sneaking furtively among the willows on the bank with what seemed to be a hatchet in his hand. More I cannot say.

'But I can be definite about one thing; while everyone was dancing the rumba and while the buffet was plying a heavy trade, it was noticed that the distance between the raft and the shore had sensibly increased. The gangplank subsided in the ooze. It was not a great distance – perhaps ten feet. But owing to the solid resistance such a large raft set up in the main current the pull was definitely outward. But as yet nobody was alarmed; indeed most of the members of the Corps thought it was part of a planned entertainment. I suppose most of the passengers on the *Titanic* turned in the night before the iceberg with just the same comfortable sense of well-being.

'Polk-Mowbray himself was concerned, it is true, though he did not lose composure. "Can't some of you secretaries get out and push it back to the bank?" he asked; but the water was already too deep. For a long minute the lighted raft hung like a water-fly on the smooth surface of the river and then slowly began to move downstream in the calm night air, the candles fluttering softly, the band playing, and the Corps dancing or smoking or gossiping, thoroughly at peace with itself. There was at this stage some hope that at the next bend of the river the whole thing would run aground on the bank, and a few of us made preparations to grab hold of the log pontoons or the overhanging willows and halt our progress. But by ill luck an eddy carried us just too far into the centre of the river and we were carried past the spit of land, vainly groping at the tips of bushes.

'By now our situation deserved serious thought. There was literally no stop now until we reached Belgrade and here – the sweat started out on me as I thought of it – the Danube joins the Sava and causes something like a tidal bore, a permanent whirlpool. While the Sava is comparatively sluggish the Danube comes down from Rumania at about fourteen knots – impossible to swim in or ford. The point of junction is just below the fortress of Belgrade, a picturesque enough spot for those on dry land . . .

'It was about five minutes before the full significance of our position began to dawn upon the Corps and by this time we were moving in stately fashion down the centre of the fairway, all lit up like a Christmas tree. Expostulations, suggestions, counter-suggestions poured from the lips of the diplomats and their wives in a dozen tongues.

'Unknown to us, too, other factors were being introduced which were to make this a memorable night for us all. Yugoslavia, as you know, was hemmed in at this time by extremely angry Communist states which kept her in a perpetual state of alarm by moving troops about on her borders, or by floating recriminatory and sometimes pornographic literature down the rivers which intersected the country – in an attempt, one imagines, to unman Serbian Womanhood, if such a thing be possible. At any rate, spy-mania was at meridian and the Yugoslav forces lived in a permanent state of alertness. There were frequent rumours of armed incursions from Hungary and Czechoslovakia . . .

'It was in this context that some wretched Serbian infantryman at an observation post along the river saw what he took to be a large armed man-of-war full of Czech paratroops in dinner jackets and ball-dresses sailing upon Belgrade, the capital. He did not wait to verify this first impression. Glaucous-eyed, he galloped into Belgrade castle a quarter of an hour later on a foam-flecked mule with the news that the city was about to be invested. The tocsin was sounded, while we, blissfully unaware of this, sailed softly down the dark water to our doom.

'It was lucky that there was only one gun in Belgrade castle. This was manned by Comrade Popovic and a scratch team of Albanian Shiptars clad in skull caps of white wool and goatskin breeches. (Fearsome to look at because of his huge moustache and shapeless physique the Shiptar is really a peaceable animal, about as quarrelsome as a Labrador and with the personality of a goldfish.) Usually it took the team about a week to load the Gun, which was a relic left behind them by the departing Visigoths or Ostrogoths – I forget which. Strictly speaking, too, it was not an offensive weapon as such but a Saluting Gun. Every evening during Ramadan it would give a hoarse boom at sunset, while a pair of blue underpants, which had been used from time immemorial as wadding for the blank charge, would stiffen themselves out on the sky.

'Nevertheless, when the news of the invasion reached Comrade Popovic he realized in a flash that the defence of the city depended entirely on him. He closed his eyes for a brief moment and saw himself receiving, in rapid succession, the Order of the Sava, The Order of St. Michael First Class, the Order of Mercy and Plenty with crossed Haystacks, and the Titotalitarian Medal of Honour with froggings. He set his platoon the task of scraping together a lethal charge capable of scattering the invaders as they came round the bend in the river. This was to be composed of a heterogeneous collection of beer bottle tops, discarded trouser buttons, cigarette-tins and fragments of discarded railway train. The aged gun was slewed round after a violent spell of man-hauling and brought to bear upon the target area.

'Meanwhile things aboard the raft were not going too well. Signs of incipient disintegration had begun to set in. Some of De Mandeville's artful trellis work had gone while the whole buffet had rather surprisingly broken off from the main body and started on a journey of its own down a narrow tributary of the river. I still remember the frozen faces of the waiters as they gazed around them despairingly like penguins on an ice-floe. Bozo's Band still kept up a pitiful simulacrum of sound but they had to keep moving position as the water was leaking along the tarpaulin and enveloping their ankles. Many of the candles had gone out. The chill of despair had begun to settle on the faces of the diplomats as the full urgency of the situation became plain to them. In their mind's eye they could hear – not to mix a metaphor – the fateful roar of the Danube water in its collision with the slow and peaceful Sava. Involuntary exclamations burst from the more voluble ladies. Was there nothing we could do? Could we not signal? Perhaps if we lit a fire . . . ? But these were counsels of despair as well they knew. I think we all felt in our bones that we should have to swim for it. The Italian Ambassador who had not swum for a quarter of a century tried a few tentative strokes in the air in a vain attempt to remember the routine. The only lucky person was Tope who had fallen asleep under the bar and was being borne off steadily down the tributary towards the sawmills where presumably he would be cut up by absent-minded Serbs and turned into newsprint – a fitting end.

'By this time we had reached the fatal bend in the river overlooked by the bastions of the castle where Pithecanthropos Popovic waited, eyes on the river, safety match at the ready. The Gun was loaded to the brim. He knew he could not afford to miss us as it would be at least a week before the raw material for another lethal charge could be gathered from the dustbins of Belgrade. It was now or never. He drew a deep ecstatic breath as he saw us come round the bend, slowly, fatefully, straight into his line of fire. He applied the safety match to the touch-hole.

'There was a husky roar and the night above us was torn by a lurid yellow flash while the still water round the raft was suddenly ripped and pock-marked by a hail of what seemed to us pretty sizeable chain-shot. Pandemonium broke out. "My God," cried the Argentine Minister, who always showed a larger White Feather than anyone else, "they're shooting at us!" He took refuge behind the massive Hanoverian frame of Madame Hess, wife of the German First Secretary. "Throw yourselves on your faces!" cried the Swiss Minister, suiting the action to the word. The Italian Ambassador refused this injunction with some hauteur. "Porca Madonna, I shall die standing up", he cried, striking an attitude with one hand on his breast.

'Though nobody was actually hurt the bombardment had carried away most of the band's instruments, half the marquee and the rest of the De Mandeville's dainty trellis-work. It had also holed an ice-box filled with tomato juice and scattered the stuff, with its fearful resemblance to blood, all over us, so that many of us looked cut to pieces. Nor did we know then that it would take Comrade Popovic a week to repeat his exploit. We expected a dozen more guns to open on us as we neared the city. Some of the ladies began to cry, and others to staunch the apparent wounds made by the flying tomato juice on their menfolk. The Argentine Minister, suddenly noticing a red stain spreading on his white dinner-jacket front cried out: "Caramba! They've got me!" and fell in a dead faint at Madame Hess's feet.

'The raft looked like a Victorian battle-piece by a master of anecdote. Some lay on their faces, some crouched behind chairs, some stood gesticulating, but all were racked with moans. It was now, too, that Polk-Mowbray turned savagely on poor De Mandeville and hissed: "Why don't you do something? Why don't you shout for help?" Obediently above the racket De Mandeville raised his pitiful female-impersonator's screams: "Help! Help!" into the enigmatic night.

'No further guns barked at us from the fort but by now the river had narrowed and its flow had increased. The raft began to spin round and round in a series of sickening rotations as it neared the fateful junction. Ahead of us we could see the blaze of searchlights and the stir of river traffic. My God, what fresh trials were awaiting us down there at the whirlpool's edge? Perhaps squads of whiskered Serbs were waiting to greet us with a hail of small-arms fire. A green-and-red rocket shot up in the farther darkness, increasing our alarm.

'Now the only people who had been of any real assistance to us in our predicament (though we did not know it then) were the chauffeurs of the Diplomatic Corps. They were mostly Serbian and virtually constituted a Corps on their own; jutting fore-heads, lowering forelocks, buck teeth, webbed hands and feet, vast outcrops of untamed hair stretching away to every skyline . . . They alone had watched our departure with alarm – with shrill ululations and inarticulate cries as they shifted their feet about in the ooze and watched the raft borne to its destruction. Moreover, they remembered what happened at the confluence of the two rivers. No sooner, therefore, were we out of sight than the chauffeurs started out for town – a long line of official limousines.

'They had the sense, moreover, to go down to the dock and alert the river police and to enlist the aid of all the inhabitants of the coal quay whose bum-boats might be of use in grounding the raft before it reached the Niagara Falls. Two police boats with searchlights and a variety of sweat-stained small-boat owners accordingly set off up the Sava to head us off. This was the meaning of the lights and rockets on the river which caused us so much alarm.

'But they had reckoned without the mean size of the raft; even with all the missing bits which had flaked off it was still the size of a ballroom floor and correspondingly heavy. The bum-boats and the river launches met us in sickening collision about four hundred yards above the river junction. We were by this time so confused and shaken as to be almost out of our minds. Most of us thought that we had been attacked by pirates, and this impression was heightened when a huge Serb picked up Madame Hess in one hand and deposited her in his bum-boat. Cries of "Rape!" went up from the Latin-American secretaries who had seen this sort of thing before. Meanwhile, half-blinded by searchlights and repeatedly knocked off their feet by the concussion of launches hitting the raft, the Swedish Embassy, in one of those sudden attacks of hysteria which afflict Nordics, decided to die to the last man rather than allow our rescuers aboard. The friendly, willing Serbs suddenly found themselves grappled by lithe young men clad in dinner jackets who sank their teeth into their necks and rolled overboard with them. A disgraceful *fracas* ensued. Despite the powerful engines of the river launches, too, the raft was irresistibly moving towards the rapids carrying not only the Flower of European Diplomacy but also a large assortment of bum-boats whose owners were letting out shrill cries and rowing in every direction but the right one.

'It was all over with us, old man. Not exactly in a flash but in series of movements like a bucking bronco. Those of us who had read Conrad's *Typhoon* felt we had been here before.

'The Danube ripped the tarpaulin off, unstapled the logs and threw everything into the air. It was lucky that there were enough logs to go round. I can't say the Diplomatic Corps looked its best sitting astride logs with the water foaming round it, but it was certainly something you don't see every day. The Argentine Minister was borne screaming off into the night and only picked up next morning ten miles down river. Indeed, the banks of the Danube as far as the town of Smog were littered with the whitening bones of Swedes and Finns and Japs and Greeks. De Mandeville was struck on the head and knocked insensible; Polk-Mowbray broke his collar bone. Draper lost a toupee which cost about a hundred pounds and was forced to go about in a beret for nearly two months.

'We could not call the roll for twenty-four hours and when we did it seemed nothing less than a miracle that we had endured no major casualties. It's the sort of thing which almost makes one Take Refuge in Religion.

'As for Benbow, he had gone on long leave by next morning and was not due back for six months. It was a tactful retreat. Polk-Mowbray himself drew the moral and adorned the tale by remarking to the Chancery: "The Great Thing in Diplomacy is Never to Over-reach Oneself." I think he had got hold of something there, even if he was just being wise after the event.'

LA VALISE

'If there is anything worse than a soprano,' said Antrobus judicially as we walked down the Mall towards his club, 'it is a mezzo-soprano. One shriek lower in the scale, perhaps, but with higher candle-power. I'm not just being small-minded, old chap. I bear the scars of spiritual experience. Seriously.' And indeed he did look serious; but then he always does. The aura of the Foreign Office clings to him. He waved his umbrella, changed step, and continued in a lower, more confidential register. 'And I can tell you another thing. If there is anything really questionable about the French character it must be its passion for *culture*. I might not dare to say this in the FO old man, but I know you will respect my confidence. You see, we are all supposed to be pro rather than anti in the Old Firm – but as for me, frankly I hate the stuff. It rattles me. It gives me the plain untitivated pip, I don't mind confessing.'

He drew a deep breath and after a pause went on, more pensively, drawing upon his memories of Foreign Service life: 'All my worst moments have been cultural rather than political. Like that awful business of *La Valise*, known privately to the members of the Corps as The Diplomatic Bag Extraordinary. Did I ever mention it? She was French Ambassadress in Vulgaria.'

'No.'

'Shall I? It will make you wince.'

'Do.'

'Well it happened while I was serving in Vulgaria some years ago; an unspeakable place full of unspeakable people. It was the usual Iron Curtain post to which the FO had exposed its soft white underbelly in the person of Smith-Cromwell. Not that he was a bad chap. He was in fact quite intelligent and had played darts for Cambridge. But he was easily led. As you know in a Communist country the Corps finds itself cut off from every human contact. It has to provide its own amusements, fall back on its own resources. And this is where the trouble usually begins. It is a strange thing but in a post like that it is never long before some dastardly Frenchman (always French) reaches for the safety-catch of his revolver and starts to introduce *culture* into our lives. Invariably.

'So it fell out with us in Sczbog. Sure enough, during my second winter the French appointed a Cultural Attaché, straight from Montmartre – the place with the big church. Fellow like a greyhound. Burning eyes. Dirty hair. A moist and Fahrenheit handshake. You know the type. Wasn't even married to his own wife. Most Questionable fellow. Up till now everything had been quiet and reasonable – just the usual round of diplomatic-social engagements among colleagues. Now this beastly fellow started the ball rolling with a public lecture – an undisguised public lecture – on a French writer called, if I understood him correctly, Flowbear. Of course we all had to go to support the French. Cultural reciprocity and all that. But as if this wasn't enough the little blackhead followed it up with another about another blasted French writer called, unless my memory is at fault, Goaty-eh. I ask you, my dear fellow, what was one to do. Flowbear! Goaty-eh! It was more than flesh and blood could stand. I myself feared the worst as I sat listening to him. The whole thing cried out for the chloroform-pad. I had of course wound up and set my features at Refined Rapture like everyone else, but inside me I was in a turmoil of apprehension. Culture spreads like mumps, you know, like measles. A thing like this could get everyone acting unnaturally in no time. All culture corrupts, old boy, but French culture corrupts absolutely. I was not wrong.

'The echoes had hardly died away when I noticed That Awful Look coming over people's faces. Everyone began to think up little tortures of their own. A whole winter stretched before us with practically no engagements except a national day or so. It was clear that unless Smith-Cromwell took a strong line the rot would set in. He did not. Instead of snorting when *La Valise* embarked on a cultural season he weakly encouraged her; he was even heard to remark that culture was a Good Thing – for the Military Attaché.

'At this time of course we also had our cultural man. Name of Gool. And he looked it. It was a clear case of Harrow and a bad third in History. But up to now we had kept Gool strictly under control and afraid to move. It could not last. He was bound to come adrift. Within a month he was making common cause with his French colleague. They began to lecture, separately and together. They gave readings with writhings. They spared us nothing, Eliot, Sartre, Emmanuel Kant – and who is that other fellow? The name escapes me. In short they gave us everything short of Mrs Beeton. I did my best to get an arm-lock on Gool and to a certain extent succeeded by threatening to recommend him for an OBE. He knew this would ruin his career and that he would be posted to Java. But by the time I had got him pressed to the mat it was too late. The whole Corps had taken fire and was burning with the old hard gem-like flame. Culture was spreading like wildfire.

'A series of unforgettable evenings now began, old boy. Each mission thought up some particularly horrible contribution of its own to this feast. The nights became a torture of pure poesy and song. An evening of hellish amateur opera by the Italians would be followed without intermission by an ear-splitting evening of yodelling from the Swiss, all dressed as edelweiss. Then the Japanese mission went beserk and gave a Noh-play of ghoulish obscurity lasting seven hours. The sight of all those little yellowish, inscrutable diplomats all dressed as Mickey Mouse, old boy, was enough to turn milk. And their voices simply ate into one. Then in characteristic fashion the Dutch, not to be outdone, decided to gnaw their way to the forefront of things with a recital of national poetry by the Dutch Ambassadress herself. This was when I began to draft my resignation in my own mind. O God! how can I ever forget Madame Vanderpipf (usually the most kind and normal of wives and mothers) taking up a stance like a grenadier at Fontenoy, and after a pause declaiming in a slow, deep – O unspeakably slow and deep – voice, the opening verses of whatever it was? Old Boy, the cultural heritage of the Dutch is not my affair. Let them have it, I say. Let them enjoy it peacefully as they may. But spare me from poems of five hundred lines beginning, '*Oom kroop der poop*'. You smile, as well indeed you may, never having heard Mrs Vanderpipf declaiming those memorable stanzas with all the sullen fire of her race. Listen!

> Oom kroop der poop
> Zoom kroon der soup
> Soon droon der oopersnoop.

'And so on. Have you got the idea? Perhaps there is something behind it all – who am I to say? All I know is that it is no joke to be on the receiving end. Specially as she would pause from time to time to give a rough translation in pidgin for Smith-Cromwell's benefit. Something like this: "Our national poet, Snugerpouf, he says eef Holland lives forever, only, how you would say?, heroes from ze soil oopspringing, yes?" It was pulsestopping, old man. Then she would take a deep breath and begin afresh.

> Oom kroop der poop
> Zoom kroon der soup.

'In after years the very memory of this recitation used to make the sweat start out of my forehead. You must try it for yourself sometime. Just try repeating '*oom kroop der poop*' five hundred times in a low voice. After a time it's like Yoga. Everything goes dark. You feel you are falling backwards into illimitable black space.

'By this time Smith-Cromwell himself had begun to suffer. He leaned across to me once on this particular evening to whisper a message. I could tell from his popping eye and the knot of throbbing veins at his temple that he was under strain. He had at last discovered what culture means. "If this goes on much longer", he hissed, "I shall confess everything."

'But this did go on; unremittingly for a whole winter. I spare you a description of the cultural offerings brought to us by the remoter tribes. The Argentines! The Liberians! Dear God! When I think of the Chinese all dressed in lamp-shades, the Australians doing sheep-opera, the Egyptians undulating and ululating all in the same breath . . . Old boy I am at a loss.

'But the real evil demon of the peace was *La Valise*. Whenever culture flagged she was there, quick to rekindle the flame. Long after the Corps was milked dry, so to speak, and had nothing left in its collective memory except nursery rhymes or perhaps a bluish limerick or two, *La Valise* was still at it. She fancied herself as a singer. She was never without a wad of music. A mezzo soprano never gives in, old boy. She dies standing up, with swelling port curved to the stars . . . And here came this beastly attaché again. He had turned out to be a pianist, and she took him everywhere to accompany her. While he clawed the piano she clawed the air and remorselessly sang. How she sang! Always a bit flat, I gather, but with a sickening lucid resonance that penetrated the middle ear. Those who had hearing-aids filled them with a kapok mixture for her recitals. When she hit a top note I could hear the studs vibrating in my dinner-shirt. Cowed, we sat and watched her, as she started to climb a row of notes towards the veil of the temple – that shattering top E, F or G: I never know which. We had the sinking feeling you get on the giant racer just as it nears the top of the slope. To this day I don't know how we kept our heads.

'Smith-Cromwell was by this time deeply penitent about his earlier encouragement of *La Valise* and at his wits' end to see her stopped. Everyone in the Chancery was in a bad state of nerves. The Naval Attaché had taken to bursting into tears at meals if one so much as mentioned a forthcoming cultural engagement. But what was to be done? We clutched at every straw; and De Mandeville, always resourceful, suggested inviting the Corps to a live reading by himself and chauffeur from the works of the Marquis de Sade. But after deliberation Smith-Cromwell thought this might, though Effective, seem Questionable, so we dropped it.

'I had begun to feel like Titus Andronicus, old man, when the miracle happened. Out of a cloudless sky. Nemesis intervened just as he does in Gilbert Murray. Now *La Valise* had always been somewhat hirsute, indeed quite distinctly moustached in the Neapolitan manner, though none of us for a moment suspected the truth. But one day after Christmas M. De Panier, her husband, came round to the Embassy in full *tenue* and threw himself into Cromwell-Smith's arms, bathed in tears as the French always say. "My dear Britannic Colleague," he said, "I have come to take my leave of you. My career is completely ruined. I am leaving diplomacy for good. I have resigned. I shall return to my father-in-law's carpet factory near Lyons and start a new life. All is over."

'Smith-Cromwell was of course delighted to see the back of *La Valise*; but we all had a soft corner for De Panier. He was a gentleman. Never scamped his *frais* and always gave us real champagne on Bastille Day. Also his dinners were dinners – not like the Swedes; but I am straying from my point. In answer to Smith-Cromwell's tactful inquiries De Panier unbosomed.

'You will never credit it, old man. You will think I am romancing. But it's as true as I am standing here. There are times in life when the heart spires upward like the lark on the wing; when through the consciousness runs, like an unearthly melody, the thought that God *really* exists, really *cares*; more, that he turns aside to lend a helping hand to poor dips *in extremis*. This was such a moment, old boy.

'*La Valise* had gone into hospital for some minor complaint which defied diagnosis. And in the course of a minor operation the doctors discovered that she was *turning into a man*! Nowadays of course it is becoming a commonplace of medicine; but at the time of which I speak it sounded like a miracle. A *man*, upon my soul! We could hardly believe it. The old caterpillar was really one of *us*. It was too enchanting! We were saved!

'And so it turned out. Within a matter of months her voice – that instrument of stark doom – sank to a bass; she sprouted a beard. Poor old De Panier hastened to leave but was held up until his replacement came. Poor fellow! Our hearts went out to him with This Whiskered Wonder on his hands. But he took it all very gallantly. They left at last, in a closed car, at dead of night. He would be happier in Lyons, I reflected, where nobody minds that sort of thing.

'But if he was gallant about this misfortune so was *La Valise elle-même*. She went on the halls, old boy, as a bass-baritone and made quite a name for herself. Smith-Cromwell says he once heard her sing "The London Derrière" in Paris with full orchestra and that she brought the house down. Some of the lower notes still made the ash-trays vibrate a bit but it was no longer like being trapped in a wind-tunnel. She wore a beard now and a corkscrew moustache and was very self-possessed. One can afford to be Over There. He also noticed she was wearing a smartish pair of elastic-sided boots. Oh, and her trade name now was Tito Torez. She and De Panier were divorced by then, and she had started out on a new career which was less of a reign of terror, if we can trust Smith-Cromwell. Merciful are the ways of Providence!

'As for poor De Panier himself, I gather that he re-entered the service after the scandal had died down. He is at present Consul-General in Blue Springs, Colorado. I'm told that there isn't much culture there, so he ought to be a very happy man indeed.'

STIFF UPPER LIP

As for the Fair Sex (said Antrobus), I am no expert, old boy. I've always steered clear. Mind you, I've admired through binoculars as one might admire a fine pair of antlers. Nearest I ever came to being enmeshed was in the *Folies Bergères* one night. Fortunately, Sidney Trampelvis was there and got me out into the night air and fanned me with his cape until my head cleared and I realized the Full Enormity of what I'd done. Without realizing it, I had proposed to a delightful little pair of antlers called Fifi and was proposing to take her back to the Embassy and force the Chaplain to gum us up together. Phew! I certainly owe Sidney a debt. We positively galloped away from the place in a horse-drawn contrivance with our opera hats crushed like puff-pastry. Sidney, who was only visiting, and who had also crossed the subliminal threshold and proposed – dear God – to a contortion-ist; Sidney was even paler than I. That night he dyed his hair green to escape identification and crossed over to Dover on the dusk packet – a bundle of nerves.

But Dovebasket in love was a strange sight. His sighs echoed through the Chancery. There were sonnets and triolets and things all over the backs of the War Office despatches. The little winged youth had certainly pinked him through the spencer. Yes, it was Angela, Polk-Mowbray's niece. I can't think why Polk-Mowbray didn't liquidate one or both of them. But then the Popular Verdict on *him* was that he needed stiffening. Yes, the stiffest thing about him was perhaps his upper lip. As for Dovebasket, I would have described him as an ensanguined poop. A spoon, my dear chap, a mere spoon. Yet love makes no distinctions. Afterwards he published a little book of his poems called *Love Songs of an Assistant Military Attaché* with a preface by

Havelock Ellis. A rum book in sooth. I remember one refrain:

> The moon gleams up there like a cuspidor
> Angela, Angela, what are we waiting for?

You get the sort of stuff? Could lead directly to Nudism. It was clear from all this that he was terribly oversexed and I for one felt that he would end in Botany Bay or the Conservative Central Office or somewhere. You see, Angela wouldn't respond to the rowel at all. Not her. Press his suit as firmly as he might the wretched chap only got the tip-tilted nose in response. It was clear that she considered him as no more than a worm-powder. And here I must add that we had all been worried about Angela, for she had been showing signs of getting one of her famous crushes on the Russian Military Attaché – Serge, or Tweed, or something by name – a bloater to boot. But of course, the worst aspect of it all was that we weren't officially fraternizing at that time with The Other Bloc. Polk-Mowbray was worried about her security. He had been frightfully alarmed to overhear an idle conversation of hers with a Pole in which she gave away – without a moment's thought – the entire lay-out of Henley Regatta, every disposition, old boy. She even drew a map of the refreshment room. I know that Henley isn't Top Secret, but it might just as easily have been the dispositions of the Home Fleet. Such lightness of speech argued ill for the Mission. One simply did not know what she mightn't reveal in this way . . . We were concerned, I might say, Quite Concerned.

Well, it so fell out that during this fruitless romance of Dovebasket's the Vulgarians invited us all to join them in pushing out the boat for the Wine Industry. They had always had a Wine Industry, mind you, but it had never been put on a proper basis before. So, very wisely, they had imported a trio of French experts and turned them loose among the bins. Within a matter of a couple of years, the whole thing had been reorganized, new cultures had been sorted out, and Vulgaria was now about to launch about twenty new wines upon the export market. Advance intelligence from old Baron Hisse la Juppe, the Military Attaché (who had practically lived down there while experiments were going on) suggested that something most promising had taken place. Vulgaria, he said (rather precariously) was on the point of exporting wines which would equal anything the French and Italians could do . . . We were incredulous, of course, but were glad to assist in the send-off of the new wines. The whole Corps accepted the invitation to the *Vin d'Honneur* with alacrity.

The day dawned bright and fair, and it was a merry party of carefree dips who took the train north to the vineyards. The whole *vieillesse dorée* of diplomacy, old man. In sparkling trim. For once, the whole thing was admirably worked out; we were carried in vine-wreathed carriages to the great main cellars of the place – more like a railway tunnel than anything, where warm candle-light glowed upon twinkling glasses and white linen; where the music of minstrels sounded among the banks of flowers . . . I must say, I was transported by the beauty of the scene. There lay the banks of labelled bottles, snoozing softly upon the trestles with the candles shining upon their new names. Our hosts made speeches. We cheered. Then corks began to pop and the wine-tasting began. One of the French specialists led us round. He tried to get us to take the thing rather too professionally – you know, shuffling it about in the mouth, cocking the chin up to the ceiling and then spitting out into a kind of stone draining-board. Well as you know, one is trained to do most things in the FO. But not to spit out good wine. No. We simply wouldn't demean ourselves by this niggardly shuffling and spitting out. We swallowed. I think you would have done the same in our place. What we were given to taste, we tasted. But we put the stuff away.

And what stuff, my dear boy. Everything that Hisse la Juppe had said proved true. What wines! Wines to set dimples in the cheeks of the soul. Some were little demure white wines, skirts lifted just above the knee, as it were. Others just showed an elbow or an ankle. Others were as the flash of a nymph's thigh in the bracken. Wines in sables, wines in mink! What an achievement for the French! Some of the range of reds struck out all the deep bass organ-notes of passions – in cultured souls like ours. It was ripping. We expanded. We beamed. Life seemed awfully jolly all of a sudden. We rained congratulations upon our hosts as we gradually wound along the great cellars, tasting and judging. What wines! I couldn't decide for myself, but after many trials fell upon a red wine with a very good nose. You see, we each had to pick one, as a free crate of it was to be given to each member of the Corps. Sort of Advertisement.

And as we went along the French specialist enchanted us by reading out from his card the descriptions of the wines which we were trying. What poetry! I must hand it to the French, though they tend to make me suspicious in lots of ways. There was one, for example, a sort of hock, which was described as *'au fruité parfait, mais présentant encore une légère pointe de verdeur nullement désagréable'*. Another was described as *'séveux et bien charpenté'*. And then there was a sort of Vulgarian Meursault which was *'parfait de noblesse et de finesse, une petite splendeur'*. I must say, for a moment one almost succumbed to culture, old man. The stuff was damned good. Soon we were all as merry as tom-tits, and I even smiled by mistake at the Bulgarian Chargé. In fact everything would have gone off like a dream if Dovebasket hadn't cut up rough and sat deliberately on the air-conditioning.

Apparently in the middle of all this bonhomie the wretched youth crept up on Angela and breathed a winged word in her ear. It was the old fateful pattern. She turned on her heel and tossing up her little chin went over to the other corner where the crapulous Serge was swigging the least significant of the wines with much smacking of the lips. It was so obvious; Dovebasket was cut as if by a whiplash. A cry of fury broke from his lips to find that she preferred this revolting foreigner who had apparently been named after an inferior British export material; he banged his fist upon the nearest table and cried out, 'If I cannot have her, nobody shall!' And all of a sudden made his way to the corner of the tunnel of love and sat down. He took a copy of Palgrave's Golden Brewery from his pocket – one of those anthologies with a monotonous-looking cover – and started to read in a huffy way. Sulks, old man, mortal sulks.

Well, we sighed and went on with our bibbing, unaware that the fellow was sitting upon our life-line, as it were. I have already said that he was mechanically-minded. Apparently he had noticed that the air-supply to the tunnel came through a sort of sprocket with a side-valve cut in a sort of gasket with a remote-control intake – how does one say these things? Anyway. Dovebasket placed his behind firmly on the air-screw, thus cutting off our oxygen supply from the outer world. It was all very well trying to suffocate his rival. But – and such is the power of passion – he was determined to suffocate the entire Corps.

Well, for ages nobody noticed anything. On we went from cask to cask, in ever-growing merriment, getting more and more courtly, with each swig. We thought that Dovebasket was just alone and palely loitering, that he would grow out of it. We didn't know that he was sitting on the very H_2SO_4 or H_2O (I never was much good at chemistry) which nourished human life in these regions. I had never thought much about air before. Apparently there is something quite essential about it. Nutritious as wine is, it cannot apparently sustain life unaided. Well, as I say, there we were unaware of the formaldehyde bubbles which were slowly crawling up the bloodstream, mounting to our brains. Suddenly I noticed that everyone seemed unwontedly hilarious, a rather ghastly sort of hilarity, mind you. Laughter, talk, music – it all seemed to have gone into a new focus.

A grimly bacchanalian note set in. I was vaguely aware that things were not as they should be but I couldn't quite put my finger on it. The first to go was Gool, the British Council man. He lay down quietly in a bed of roses and passed out, only pausing to observe that he could feel the flowers growing over him. We ignored him. The music had got rather ragged at the edges. People were drinking on rather desperately now and talking louder than ever. Somewhere in the heart of it all there was a Marked Discomfort. People seemed suddenly to have aged, bent up. You could begin to see how they would look at ninety if they lived that long. The chiefs of mission had gone an ashen colour. As if they had worn their expressions almost down to the lining. It is hardly believable what a difference air can make to dips, old man.

And now it was that knees began to buckle, stays to creak, guy-ropes to give. Still, in courtly fashion, people began to look around them for something to lean on. Yes, people everywhere began to strap-hang, still talking and laughing, but somehow in a precarious way. Polk-Mowbray had gone a distinctly chalky colour and had difficulty in articulating; the Argentine Minister had quite frankly started to crawl towards the entrance on all fours.

It was Serge, I think, who first noticed the cause of our plight. With a bound he was at Dovebasket's side crying, 'Please to remove posterior from the breathing,' in quite good Satellite English. Dovebasket declined to do so. Serge pulled him and received a knee in the chest. Dovebasket settled himself firmly once more and showed clearly that he wasn't letting any more air in that week. Serge seized a wicker-covered bottle of the Chianti type and tapped him smartly on the crown. Dovebasket was not going to be treated like a breakfast egg by his hated rival. He dotted him back. This was fatal. One could see at once how wars break out. Poland and Rumania came to the Assistance of Serge, while Canada and Australia answered the call of the Mother Country. It looked like some strange Saturnalia, armed dips circling each other with wicker-covered bottles.

But as the fighting spread, Dovebasket got shifted from his perch and the life-giving H_2SO_4 began to pour once more into the cave. It was only just in time, I should say. The cellar now looked like a series of whimsical details from a Victorian canvas – I'm thinking of 'Kiss Me Hardy' with Nelson down for the count in the Victory's cockpit. Some were kneeling in pleading postures. Some were crawling about in that painstaking way that beetles do when they are drunk on sugar-water. Others had simply keeled over among the flowers. The musicians drooped over their timbrels without enough oxygen between them for a trumpet-call or a groggy drum-tap. Then all of us, suddenly realizing, set up a shout and hurled ourselves towards the life-distributing oxygen pump.

With your permission I will draw a veil over the disgraceful scenes that ensued among the combatants. Dovebasket was knocked out. The Canadian Air Attaché had a collar-bone bruised. The egregious Serge escaped unscathed. A number of bottles were broken. Such language. Life has its ugly side, I suppose. But the main thing was that the Corps lived again,

. . . the Argentine Minister had quite frankly started to crawl
towards the entrance on all fours.

breathed again, could hold up its aching head once more. But one is hardly trained to live dangerously. Nevertheless, I noticed that not one dip failed to make a note of the wine of his choice. It would have been too much to miss that free crate. Some, in default of pencil and paper, had managed to scribble on their dickeys with lipstick. Polk-Mowbray, though beaten to his knees, nevertheless had the presence of mind to write Stella Polaris 1942 on his. Bloody, but relatively unbowed, you see.

And, as a matter of fact, after prayers the next day it was he who summed it all up rather neatly by saying: 'And remember that in Peace, in War, in Love and in Diplomacy one thing is needful. I do not, I think, need to tell you what that is.'

He didn't. It would have been labouring the point. We knew only too well. The Stiff Upper Lip.

THE IRON HAND

Have you ever noticed (said Antrobus) that people called Percy are almost invariably imbeciles? Perhaps the name confers a fateful instability upon the poor souls; perhaps it is chosen as the most appropriate for those who, from birth, show all the signs of being lathe-turned morons . . . Anyway it is a fact. Hearing the name I know I need never look at the face. I am sure of the ears spread to the four winds like banana leaves, sure of the lustreless eyes, the drooling mouth, hammer-toes and so on . . . Percy is as Percy looks in my experience.

Nor was Percy, the Embassy second-footman, any exception. In fact to call him a footman was an insult to what is, after all, a *métier*. He was a superannuated potboy with the sort of face one sees slinking out of cinemas in places like Sidcup and Penge – idle, oafish and conceited. He spent hours tending the spitcurl on his receding forehead and complacently ogling the house-maids. He rode a bicycle round and round the flower-beds until Polk-Mowbray (bird-watching from his office) became giddy and ordered him to desist. He whistled with a dreadful monotonous shrillness. He chewed gum with a sickening rotary action that turned the beholder's stomach.

Well, when Drage went on leave the domestic arrangements of the Embassy were confided to this junior Quasimodo, and that is how the business of the iron hand came about. Normally Percy was never allowed to touch either the Embassy plate or the suit of armour which stood in the Conference Room and which we used to call 'The White Knight'. Personally I hated the thing, though Drage loved it dearly. It was always giving us frights during Secret Conferences. Once the beaver came down with a clang just as Polk-Mowbray was about to Come To A Decision and we all got a dreadful start. On another occasion smoke was seen curling out of its mouth and the cry of 'Spy' went up from one and all. Trampelvis had dropped a cigar-end into it. After this I had it moved into the hall. Once a month Drage used to take it apart and polish it up. Now Percy had his glaucous eye fixed firmly upon 'The White Knight', and no sooner had Drage left than he at once began to fool around with the thing.

He put the headpiece on and scared the housemaids by gargling at them through the buttery hatch after dark. He even went for a twilight ride on his bicycle dressed in the thing – out of one gate and in at the other – which made the startled Vulgarian sentries rub their eyes. Why they didn't shoot him I don't know. It must have seemed clear evidence that the Secret Service was going over on to the offensive – and one little arpeggio on a sub-machine gun would have saved us so much subsequent trouble . . .

Well, these benighted pranks went on until one day Percy met his Waterloo. After a successful appearance as Hamlet's father he regained the buttery one day, panting happily, and started to divest himself of helm and codpiece in time to serve a pre-dinner Martini in the sitting room. Judge the poor mawk's surprise when he found that the right hand wouldn't unscrew according to plan. All the wrenching and pulling in the world could not budge it. In a flash he realized that unless he cut along the dotted line this grotesque mailed fist was with him for life. The press-stud or what-have-you was jammed against the demi-quiver of the bassinet, more or less. The first I heard of it was a noise which suggested that someone was trying to shoe a mettlesome carthorse in the Residence – rustic, yet somehow out of keeping with Polk-Mowbray's ways. It didn't seem natural. It didn't fit into Our World. Listening more carefully I thought I heard the sound of human groans, and I was not wrong. The cry for a certified obstetrician had already been raised.

Percy was sobbing like a donkey, surrounded by frightened housemaids. He realized that he was dished. There he sat on the three-legged stool in the buttery, bathed in tears, and holding up this expensive-looking piece of ironmongery in dumb appeal. 'Wretched oaf!' I cried. 'You have been told a hundred times not

to touch "The White Knight".' I pulled and tugged, but it was no
go; the iron boxing-glove was stuck clean as a cavalry boot.
Various fruitless suggestions were made, various attempts to
divest him were carried out. In vain. I took him into the
Chancery in search of qualified advice. Spalding tried, De
Mandeville tried. We pushed and pulled and heaved in unison.
Percy sobbed more loudly. But the thing refused to yield. Polk-
Mowbray and a couple of archivists made their appearance,
intrigued by the noises from a normally sedate Chancery. They
brought fresh blood and fresh impetus to his rescuers. While
Polk-Mowbray stood on his chest we formed a human chain –
like getting the Lowestoft Lifeboat in – and tried to wrest the
article from him by brute force. It was no go. A little more and
we should have shredded Frederick. A private socket would
have given. 'There's no need to yell so,' said Spalding angrily.
'We are only trying to help you.' We desisted panting and had
another conference. Dovebasket summoned the Embassy chauffeurs and took counsel with them. Now plans were formulated
involving expensive and bizarre equipment – for they planned to
saw their way in with a hacksaw and so deliver the lad. But they
punctured him. Then Polk-Mowbray boldly tried to hammer the
thing off with a croquet mallet. The noise was deafening, the
result nil. I must say those medieval farriers, artificers – or
whatever they were called – knew their business. It didn't look
much, this olde worlde gauntlet, but heavens how it stuck. Percy
was by now very much frightened and perhaps slightly bruised
around the edges. We plied him with bonded gin to bring the
roses back. There he sat in Spalding's swivel-chair, letting out a
moan from time to time, and drinking thirstily. Occasionally one
of us would have a new idea and advance upon him, whereupon
he would swivel wildly in order to avoid further pain. In this
way he dealt Butch Benbow a backhand stroke with his glove
across the shoulders which felled our redoubtable Naval Attaché
and kept him down for the count. More gin, more moans. There
seemed to be no way out of the *impasse*. Time was running out.
Guests were expected. 'I've a good mind to dress you up in the
rest of this thing and send you back to your mother by air!' cried
Polk-Mowbray in a transport of fury. I felt for him.

The awful thing was that the Dutch were due to dine with us that evening. It always seemed to be the fate of the Dutch to be invited on crisis evenings. That evening was a real *kermesse héroique*. Percy was a poor butler at the best of times but tonight he bordered on the really original. He shambled round and round the room sniffing, half anaesthetized by gin and . . . well, you can imagine our guests' faces when a mailed hand appeared over their shoulder holding a soup-plate. They *must* have felt that there was something uncanny about it. Clearly they longed to pop a question but the Iron Laws of the Corps forbade it. They held their curiosity in leash. They were superb. Normally Percy always got his thumb in the soup – but the thumb this evening was an iron one. I shudder to recall it. Yet by a superhuman effort we remained calm and Talked Policy as coolly as we could. The old training dies hard. Somehow we managed to carry it off. Yet I think our hosts felt themselves to be in the presence of irremediable tragedy. They pressed our hands in silent sympathy as we tucked them into their cars. All of a sudden one felt terribly alone again – alone with the Iron Hand . . .

Well, my dear fellow, everyone had a go at that blasted hand – the Chaplain, the cipher staff, finally the doctor. The latter wanted to heat the whole thing up with a blowtorch until the press-stud expanded but that would have incinerated Percy. By this time, of course, I hardly cared what they did to him. I would willingly have amputated the arm from somewhere just above the waist, myself. But meanwhile an urgent appeal had gone out to the Museum for a professor of armour to advise us; but the only available specialist in chain-mail was away in Italy on leave. He would not return for another two days. Two days! I know that it doesn't sound a great deal. But in the middle of the night Percy found that he had lost all trace of feeling in the arm. It had got pins and needles. He sat up in bed, haunted by a new terror. It seemed to him that gangrene had perhaps set in; he had heard the doctor muttering something about the circulation of the blood . . . He bounded down the stairs into the Residence roaring like a lion and galloped into Polk-Mowbray's bedroom waving the object. Our esteemed Chief of Mission, after the nervous strain of that evening, had turned in early, and was enjoying a spell of blameless slumber. Awakened by this apparition, and being unable to understand a word of Percy's gibberish, he jumped to the purely intuitive conclusion that a fire had broken out upstairs. It was a matter of moments to break glass and press button. Woken by that fateful ringing the Embassy fire squads swept gallantly into life, headed by Morgan and Chowder, pyjama-clad and in steel helmets. Just how Percy and his Ambassador escaped a thorough foam-bath that night is a mystery to me. Neither seemed very coherent to the gallant little band of rescuers as they swept through the dining-room with their sprinklers and up the stairs.

At last order was restored and the doctor summoned, who did much to soothe Percy's fears. But he did on the other hand take a serious view of the pins and needles. The circulation was being impeded by the gauntlet apparently. Percy must somehow keep the blood flowing in it – keep the circulation going – until help from the outer world arrived. How? By banging it, if you please, banging it repeatedly on anything that was to hand, banging it day and night lest the gangrene set in. I tell you, my dear chap, that that fateful banging, which lasted two whole days and nights, rings in my ears even now. Banging on the walls, the buttery table, on the floor. Neither work nor sleep was possible. An army of poltergeists could not have done half as well. Bang, bang, bang . . . now loud and slow, now hollow and resonant, now sharp and clear. Day and night the banging haunted us until at last the Professor appeared. We received him with tears of entreaty in our eyes.

He took a look at Percy and nodded sagely. He knew, it appeared, all about these press-studs. He applied some olive oil on a feather to the relevant joints, tapped twice with his pince-nez and Presto: Percy was free. It seemed almost too good to be true – all that silence. A united sigh went up from us all – a sigh such as I have never heard from dips before or since. Silence at last descended on us, the silence of a normal embassy oozing along at the normal cruising speed. No longer the goods' yards at Swindon, no longer a branch of Bassett-Lowke, no longer a boiler-makers' jamboree in Sheffield. No. Just HM Embassy as ever was, as ever would be in future, we hoped. But just to make assurance doubly sure Polk-Mowbray had the arms taken off the suit of armour and sent home. I can't say it improved the appearance of 'The White Knight'; but then it was questionable whether anything ever could.

SOMETHING À LA CARTE?

The tragedy of Mungo Piers-Foley is one (said Antrobus) which should give every Thoughtful Person Pause. It did me. It still does. By the purest inadvertency he found himself cast into the Bottomless Pit. He was a bit absentminded that day. Yet what happened to him could happen to any of us.

Mungo was posted to us from the Blues as Military Attaché, and he was a gallant and carefree young colonel, full of the spice of life. You felt that he had a rich inner nature if only he could be persuaded to open his mouth. He was one of those mournful cylindrical men with hair parted in the middle – men who say little but think a lot. Yet who knows what they think? I don't. But he was an officer and a gentleman of unblemished reputation and a sportsman to boot. Not only to boot, to saddle as well. He had what is known as a splendid seat. He rode to hounds. However pointless the point-to-point, Mungo would be there, clearing hurdle after hurdle on his thoroughbred mule. He played polo without ever once hitting his horse. Myself I don't know much about horses, and what little I know seems to me singularly charmless. The last time I went hacking with Polk-Mowbray I got left in a tree for roughly the same reasons as Absalom. But that is neither here nor there . . .

Mungo had won a huge collection of cups and saucers which he wore on his mantelpiece. He shot. He dynamited fish. An all-round sportsman if ever there was one. We were proud of him in the Mission. All this, of course, only made his tragedy harder cheese than ever. It happened while he was in Paris for a week to help reorganize the NATO cavalry to face the threat of a rocket age. On the morning of his return he lurched into my office looking like a lot of overlooked washing-up. 'Antrobus,' he said, 'hear my story. I am finished, old thing, absolutely finished. I've just put in my resignation and left Polk-Mowbray in tears.' He sat down and fumbled for one of my cigars.

'It happened while I was in Paris,' he said. 'Quite inadvertent, the whole dashed thing. It could have happened to anyone. I popped into the Octagon for a bite. It wasn't until the *addition* came that I realized. Old man, *I had eaten a piece of horse!*'

I sprang up, startled. 'You *what*?' I cried incredulously, realizing that I was in the presence of tragedy.

'Horse,' he repeated wearily, passing his hand over his forehead. 'As I live, Antrobus, a slice carved from a gee-gee. It all seems like a horrible dream. Yet I must say it cut quite sweetly and the sauce was so dashed good that I didn't realize it. It was only when the bill came that the whole of my past life flashed before my eyes. Dear God – a horse! And I a Colonel in the Blues! I was so surprised you could have poured me out with a spoon.'

I groaned in sympathy. He gave a harsh cracked laugh and went on. 'To think of it, I who have lived for, and practically on, horses. The irony of it all. To find myself sitting there, involuntarily wrapped round a succulent slice of fetlock, feeling the world's biggest bounder. And with a touch of mustard, too.' He shuddered at the memory.

'But surely,' I said, looking as always for the Silver Lining, 'you are hardly to be blamed, Mungo. Surely you could have absorbed just one slice and then Hushed Everything Up? No one could find it in his heart to blame you.'

He shook his head sadly. 'I thought of that,' he said, 'but my conscience wouldn't give me any rest, Antrobus. After all, here I am, a founder-member of the Society For The Prevention Of Everything To Nags. Old Boy, I was largely instrumental in getting all those country houses set aside for aged horses, for getting them into the Health Service, for getting them painted by Munnings before they Passed On. Why, we were hoping to get one into Parliament this year . . . How could I strike my colours, go back on my basic principles? I admit I thought of it. After all, I have eaten many strange things in unguarded moments. I once ate some smoked grandmother in the Outer Celebes, but that was to save the regimental goat. And once at Government

'. . . Water-Rat Flambé . . .'

House in Gibraltar I *think* I ate a portion of infant monkey. But it was never proved. The ADC refused to confess. But all this is a far cry from horses, old chap. A different world. No, I confess that I sobbed aloud as I paid that bill.'

For a moment he was silent, and then went on. 'After that, Antrobus, there came an endless chain of sleepless nights. I brooded, old man. No peace. At times I thought I might go and throw myself on the mercy of Elizabeth David, confessing everything to her frankly, hiding nothing, asking for absolution. But when I mugged up her books I found no references to anything more questionable than eels or bloater paste – revolting enough, but mundane compared to what I was up against. No, there was no way out. I realized that I should have to Face the Music. So I did. I confess it hurt. I resigned from Whites and Boodles. I had myself crossed off every Stud Book in the Shires. The Athenaeum will see me no more. I even closed my account with the Army, Navy and Air-Force Stores. I transferred my overdraft. I confessed all to the Pytchley and did a public penance at Hurlingham. Then I broke my saddle over my knee . . . and all was over. I am a broken man, Antrobus. I simply came back to collect my gongs and brasses. I only popped in to say good-bye. I somehow felt you would understand.'

I was deeply moved. But what could I say to comfort and console poor Mungo? Little enough in all conscience. He still had a fortnight to carry his bat until a replacement arrived and all this time he spent in strict purdah, refusing all invitations. There was only one little incident which, in the light of subsequent events, seems to me significant. It proved how deeply he had been marked by this Major Experience. His inhibitions had begun to slough off. De Mandeville reported that Mungo had been seen in a local hotel dining on *octopus*. I could hardly believe it. *Octopus!* The stuff that comes like ectoplasm! But this was the only straw in the wind. After that, silence closed in. Then Mungo left us and passed out of memory. As the years went by I often thought of him with a twinge of compassion. Doubtless he was in some far-enough-flung colony to dine openly on yams and white mice. I saluted his gallantry in my heart.

But now here is the grisly sequel to my tale. Spalding used to go to Kenya every year to see his family and shoot a bit. One year he went up-country on *safari*. In the heart of the jungle, in a clearing, before a modest hut of wattle, he came upon a dinner-jacketed figure having a pre-prandial. 'Mungo!' he cried. Yes, it was Mungo. He had hidden his shame in that remote corner. They embraced warmly and Spalding was glad to see that his character still had a few fibres intact – for he was correctly dressed for dinner. They sat down on camp-stools and discussed a two-to-one Martini which Mungo mixed with all his old flair. Though he had aged he still looked fairly steady on his pins, and he still made the sort of Martini which fairly whistles through the rigging. Heartening signs, these.

It was only when the brain-fever birds began to call and the little radio in the corner struck eight o'clock that Spalding Suddenly Understood that it wasn't, it couldn't be, the old Mungo . . . For his host said, quite distinctly: 'Why not stay and have pot-luck with me tonight? We have elephant for dins.' *Elephant!*

Spalding paled – he had been very strictly brought up. Was it possible that Mungo was sitting out here in the wilds gorging himself on elephant? (And if so, how was it done? It must take ages to marinate?) He gulped loudly. 'Did I understand you to say elephant, Mungo?' he said.

'Yes,' said Mungo, with a kind of loose grin. 'You see, old boy, there is no such thing as a *cuisine* in Africa. Once one leaves the Old Country one achieves a kind of Universality, a Oneness with Nature. HERE EVERYTHING IS EDIBLE.' He spread his arms to the night, knocking over his glass. 'If you don't like elephant,' he went on, 'I can organize squirrel or chipmunk or boa-constrictor. It's all one. I just send out a little man with a blow-pipe and it's all yours.'

Spalding shuddered and muttered a prayer under his breath. 'Yes,' went on Mungo, 'I gave away my Boulestin and both my Elizabeth Davids. They are no use here except for missionaries who have Outworn Concepts. Personally I use Buffon's Natural History to give me ideas for my meals. Why, just to leaf through Section One (Primates) stimulates the appropriate juice, gives one an appetite. I say, you've turned awfully pale. You aren't ill, are you?'

SOMETHING À LA CARTE?

'No, no,' said Spalding, 'it is simply the kerosene light shining on my rather high and pale forehead.'

Mungo settled himself on his camp-stool and said: 'Yes, old boy. If once the readers of *The Times* found out just how Edible everything is, it would be all up with the Wine and Food Society.' Then in a slow, dreamy voice, full of naked *luxe* and *volupté*, he began to recite softly: 'Leeches *à la rémoulade* . . . Giraffe *Truffée aux Oignons* . . . Boa-constrictor *Chasseur* . . . *Ragoût de Flamingo* with *Water-Rat Flambé* . . .' He was sunk in a deep trance.

Spalding could bear it no longer. He tip-toed out of the clearing and ran like a madman in the direction of Nairobi . . .

Now I didn't tell you this story (said Antrobus) simply to upset you. No. Moreover, I hope you won't repeat it. I should hate it to get back to the Household Cavalry. It simply illustrates the sort of thing one is up against in the Service. The next Christmas, when my Aunt Hetty asked me to choose two quotations for a sampler she was making me, it was really with Mungo in mind that I made my choice. One text reads: 'By their Menus shall ye know them.' And the other: 'Nothing Exceeds like Excess' . . .

I trust you take my point?

THE SWAMI'S SECRET

I told you (said Antrobus) about the Naval Attaché and his definite leanings towards the occult? I thought I had. I don't think, however, that I ever told you about the business of the Swami. Well, the whole of my first winter old Butch Benbow, as he was laughingly called, was working away like hell on reincarnation. Breathing exercises in this office, squinting at the tip of his tongue for hours at a time until his PA nearly went out of her mind. He even took to holding his breath during the duller staff conferences and letting it out with a swish. This wasn't reassuring. His valet said that during the lunch interval he often sat cross-legged on the lawn with a begonia on his navel, frankly and openly meditating – but this may have been an exaggeration. Anyway, he had it bad, and he was nothing if not dogged. Indeed doggedness was clearly marked in his horoscope, he said. There was no mention of drunkenness or indecent exposure. Just the doggedness. Mind you, I myself doubted the wisdom of all this spiritual strain upon a nature which, I thought, was of a more spirituous cast, but . . . I held my peace. Even when he sprained a rib I said nothing.

Then one morning he came into my office and I was staggered by the change in his appearance. He walked like an aged and broken man. He was ashen pale. At first I put this down to the fact that we had all dined at the Burmese Legation the night before where they had served venison so rare as almost to lift one off the ground. But I was wrong. 'Antrobus,' he said, 'I'm ruined, old man. Dished. My blasted swami is coming out by air.'

'Your swami?' I echoed. He nodded and gulped.

'I've been taking reincarnation lessons by post from an Indian swami. Up to now he's simply been a Box Number in the Edgware Road, old man. Name of Anaconda Veranda. And jolly fruitful it's been up to now. But I wasn't prepared for a telegram saying that he was coming out to visit me and study my spiritual progress at first hand. He is arriving this afternoon.'

'Well what's wrong with that?' I said, looking for the Silver Lining. 'I bet you are the first dip to have a private swami. Everyone will be mad with envy in the Corps.' He groaned and moved from side to side, as if he were representing Colic in a charade. He said:

'My dear chap, surely you know that all swamis are little naked men in spectacles walking around with a goat on a string? What could I do with him here? I couldn't take him to cocktails with the French. I should become the laughing-stock of the whole Corps if I were seen bowling about attached to a man in a loin-cloth. The press would certainly get hold of it. What would the Admiralty say if they saw a picture of me in the Navy Weekly? You know how materialistic they are. It would mean the China Station again, and my liver wouldn't stand it.'

I took a deep breath. I began to see his point. A loin-cloth is a tricky thing in diplomacy; in the hands of the Ill-Disposed it could become a Secret Weapon. I pondered.

'Well,' I said at last, 'you will have to try and Carry It Off somehow. Pretend he's a cousin of somebody important like Noël Coward or Bruce Lockhart. It's the only chance.' But he was sunk in gloom and hardly heeded me. 'And then there's another thing,' he said gloomily. 'I'm supposed to be living on goat's milk – not unsweetened condensed touched up with Gordon's Dry. Somehow I couldn't bring myself to keep a goat in the house. They smell so. I expect he'll give me a dressing down on spiritual grounds when he finds out. And honestly, Antrobus, I don't see myself passing him off as a relation, do you?' To be honest I didn't really; but what was to be done? The plane had already left London with Butch's little spiritual adviser aboard. We would have to face up to reality. I confess my heart ached for old Butch.

But if he was pale now, my colleague, he was a great deal paler that afternoon as he got into the official car and set off for the airport to meet his swami. I didn't blame him. The dew of death had settled on his somewhat receding brow. The poor chap could see himself socially dished as well as spiritually pooped.

Imagine his relief, however, when out of the aircraft stepped – not a naked Dravidian leading a quarantined goat – but the most poised and charming of Indian princelings, clad in beautifully cut clothes and wearing a turban with an emerald the size of a goitre in it. Anaconda Veranda was perfectly delightful, a Man Of The World, a Gentleman. Butch nearly fainted with relief as he listened to his perfect English, his exquisite English – rather better than Butch's own brand of the stuff. Could this be the swami he so much dreaded? Butch swooned back in his car muttering prayers of thanksgiving. By the time he reached the Embassy with his swami he was a changed man. He was swollen with pride, gloating almost.

I must say I found Veranda – everyone found him – perfectly delightful. It seems that he had been at Oxford with all of us – though strangely enough nobody remembered him. But he was as unbashfully Balliol as it is possible to be. And far from receiving the acid drop Butch found himself the most sought-after man in the Corps. All because of his swami. Veranda danced beautifully, was modest, wise, witty and gentle; he also played the flute to distraction which endeared him frightfully to Polk-Mowbray. He was even spiritually accommodating and let Butch know that in certain stages of spiritual development the odd touch of gin in unsweetened condensed is just the job and has the unofficial approval of the Dalai Lama. Butch was in ecstasies. So were we all.

Veranda did quite a bit of drawing-room occultism, turning tables and telling fortunes until the Ladies of the Corps were almost mad with flattery and apprehension. He hypnotized Drage and took an endless succession of hard-boiled eggs out of his nose. He predicted Collin's appointment to China. He told Dovebasket the size of his overdraft to two places of decimals. My dear chap, he was a Man of Parts. In next to no time he had most of the Ambassadresses pleading openly for spiritual instruction while the Heads of Mission, mad with envy, were cabling their head office for swamis to be sent out on approval by air freight. Polk-Mowbray even conceived the idea of creating a special post of Senior Spiritual Adviser to the Embassy and appointing Veranda to it. Just to keep him with us. But I think the Chaplain intervened and quashed the idea. Polk-Mowbray sulked a good deal after this.

Well, for a whole season Veranda occupied the social spotlight, to our intense pride. He dined here, he dined there. He was put up for the OBE and the Croix De Guerre – and quite a lot of other decorations. As a social draw he was unequalled, a human magnet. And of course Butch went up to the top of the class. He had to engage a private secretary to keep his now bulging Engagements Book and head off mere climbers with the Retort Civil (but Cutting). He was a happy man.

But now comes the *dénouement* – which poor Polk-Mowbray probably refers to as 'the pay-off' nowadays. It happened quite suddenly and gracefully. I must say that Veranda must have made a close social study of the Corps and its movements. He chose one of those ghastly holidays – was it Labour Day? – when he could be sure that the whole Corps was sitting on a dais in the main square of the town, perspiring freely and watching the infantry defile – if that is the word. Yes, it was beautifully conceived, perfectly timed. He started by borrowing the official car and a dozen of De Mandeville's pigskin suitcases. In leisurely fashion, and with that irresistibly endearing smile which had won so many friends and influenced so many people – he made a tour of the Embassies cleaning them out with judgement and discretion. Such selectivity, old man. Only the best seemed to be good enough. Just the top jewellery like Polk-Mowbray's dress studs, Angela's tiara . . . the top treasures like the original Leonardo drawings in the Argentine Legation, the two Tiepolos *chez* the Italians, the first edition of Hamlet in Spalding's library, the two Mycenaean brooches of the Greek Ambassadress. He even took Nelson's Dress Sword which was Butch's only real treasure and on which he always made toast in the winter. And with all this stuff safely stowed in his saddle-bags the fellow evaporated, snuffed himself out, dematerialized . . . Well, old boy, you can imagine the rumpus. What an eruption! At first one hardly believed it. Surprised! You could have sluiced us down with frangipani. Many was the hanging head, many the pallid glance. Poor Butch found himself at the bottom of the form again – so did we all. For this terrible house-guest had become firmly identified with our Mission. I don't know how we lived through the next few months. Butch's swami was never traced, nor was any single item from all this cultural boodle. Somewhere among the bazaars of India these treasures must be on sale. One blenches to think of it.

It took Butch years to live down his swami. But the worst of it all was that he never finished his reincarnation course; somehow he hadn't the heart to go on. Nor has he ever had the heart or the social courage to try another swami. And as he hasn't mastered the drill he lives – so I understand from common friends – in perpetual terror of being reincarnated as a soldier.

THE UNSPEAKABLE ATTACHÉ

It was (said Antrobus) a bit before your time – mercifully for you. The creature was posted just before you arrived. Now of this fellow, Trevor Dovebasket (he was then assistant Military Attaché), I have only this to say: it was clear that the youth was in league with the Devil. Some fearful Faustian compact had taken place. You could tell from his appearance – eyebrows meeting in the middle. It was clear from the way that he bit his nails that he read *Popular Mechanics* in secret. More, his office was always full of meccano and string. He was always tampering with electrical circuits, fuses, and using that beastly sticky stuff and so on. A really vicious streak. One day Polk-Mowbray got a terrific electric shock off his telephone. Then some Juliets exploded under the noses of the Rotary Club causing grave loss of morale. It was never proved, of course, but I knew . . . Something told me it was Dovebasket.

He was in league with the Devil on one side and De Mandeville on the other. Together they organized a form of beetle-racing in the Chancery. Beetles with electromagnets tied to their tails, if you please. Imagine my concern. The beetles were named after us. They made a book and encouraged betting wholesale. Dolly Pusey, the new cipherine, gambled away a year's unearned increments and most of the fruits of the FO Pension Scheme in a matter of minutes. When I found out I had no option but to return her to London. But that was not all . . .

They invented an electric train for serving food and sold the idea to Drage as a labour-saving device. The train ran on to the dining-table and stopped before the diners with a plate on each carriage. On the face of it it seemed ingenious. It was worked by buttons from Polk-Mowbray's place. Mind you, I had my doubts. But as there was an Electrical Trades Union Conference and we had some of its members to lunch Polk-Mowbray (who had a childish steak) thought he would impress them with his little toy. You have guessed? It was not until the *Bombe Surprise* was loaded that the machinery went wrong. There was a frightful accident, the train was derailed into our laps, and the *Bombe* (a marvellous creation on which Drage had spent all night) lived up to its name . . . De Mandeville got Number One Field Punishment. He had to feed the goldfish in the Residence for a month.

Well, this is only to show you what I was up against with this fellow Dovebasket. At this time the Corps was going through one of its Little Phases. Dips are a somewhat emulous tribe as you know, always trying to vie with one another. That winter it was dogs. The Hungarians led off. Their Labour Attaché suddenly appeared with some colossal greyhounds from the Steppes. He allowed himself to be towed about in public by them wearing a somewhat fanciful air. At once everyone got emulous. In a matter of weeks the dog market was booming. Everyone had dogs of various sizes and shapes: huge ones, little ones, squashed-looking ones and ones that looked like cold rissoles. The French went in for topiary jobs, the Italians for the concertina shape, the British for those great torpid brutes which carry Hennessy's Brandy round in artful little barrels. I forget their names. They rescue people from snowdrifts by licking their faces and dealing out a much-needed tot at the right time. Horrible. The Albanians produced some green-fanged sheep-dogs so fierce that they had to be kept tied to trees in the grounds and fed by a system of underarm bowling until a shepherd was found who understood their natures. He took them for walks on a length of steel hawser.

Well, this was all very well, had not Polk-Mowbray been fired by the idea of a Diplomatic Dog-Show. He was always easily led and this fellow Dovebasket fired him with thoughts of winning a first prize in the barrel-pushing class. I viewed the whole thing with concern, but I could not guess from which quarter the blow might fall. Anyway, they worked out a splendid dog-show at which every Mission would win the first prize of its class and all

our honours be simultaneously saved. Rosettes, buttons, mark-
ing-cards – everything was thought out. A firm of dog-biscuit
manufacturers was persuaded to put up some rather depressing
prizes in the form of dog-statuettes in pressed steel which De
Mandeville painted with gold leaf to make look more expensive.
The Town Hall was engaged for the *venue* and the press was fed
with a great deal of advance information in the form of
newsflashes which it did not use. Speeches were carefully
worked up containing the requisite number of Tactful Phrases
about Everything. The ladies of the Corps decided to make it a
contest of dresses as well as dogs. Many were the clever little
creations run up overnight, many the models flown from Paris.
The air was full of excitement. It was the first Spring engagement. Sewing machines hummed night and day. The Minister
For Interior was invited to give away the prizes – there was one
for each Chief of Mission. Polk-Mowbray went through agonies
of excitement practising his Few Words Of Thanks in the
Residence pier-glass. Altogether it looked like a pleasurable and
harmonious afternoon. But . . . there was a look in Dovebasket's
eye I disliked. Could it be, I wondered, that the fellow was Up
To Something? One never knew. I confess that there was a still
small voice within me which whispered 'Something is bound to
give' as I studied the (I must say) very creditable lay-out of the
Town Hall, gay with the flags of every nation and made brilliant
by the courtly presence of Our Ladies in their prettiest frocks.
The day was fine and sunny. The dogs were extremely even
tempered, wagging their grotesque stumps and coloured rib-
bons as the solemn group of judges circulated marking down
points on their embossed cards. Cocktails were coming up thick
and fast.

It was at this point that I distinctly heard De Mandeville say in
the hoarse undertone. 'Let her go now, Dovie.' Together the two
retreated to a high stand above the *mêlée* while a look of intense
interest came over their faces. Dovebasket appeared to have a
cold and put a handkerchief to his face. He appeared to blow his
nose. Suddenly a quiver of anguish appeared to run through the
canine population like a wind in corn. The Albanian sheep-dogs
gave one long quivering howl like an Alban Berg violin solo and

. . . the British [went] for those great torpid brutes which carry
Hennessy's Brandy round in artful little barrels.

then . . . all hell broke loose. These peaceable amiable dogs suddenly turned upon their masters and the judges, seething with an inexplicable rage. They turned upon one another. Cries and tumult arose. Stands were overturned. The sheep-dogs went into action against the Labradors, the Airedales against the Fox terriers. Owners were dragged hither and thither by their leashes which got inextricably mixed up with chairs and legs and dips. Bites of all sizes and depths were registered. Blood began to flow, tempers to rise. The Russians began to shake their fists. The Minister was bitten in his . . . seat of office. Polk-Mowbray lost a spat to a shaggy mixed-up Borzoi. Lap-dogs squealed like piccolos, the bigger brutes bayed, the diplomats moaned, positively moaned.

In a single bound I was at Dovebasket's side. I whipped the handkerchief from his face. 'Unmasked,' I hissed. It was just as I thought. He was blowing hard upon one of those whistles which, while inaudible to the human ear, produced a high-pitched buzz calculated to unnerve dogs. 'It was simply an experiment,' he said with a sickly smile, 'De Mandeville betted me an even tenner that my whistle wouldn't work.'

'Experiment!' I cried. 'Look around you, you wretched youth'. The scene was a terrible one to witness. I have not seen anything to equal it – except perhaps once when someone released a grass-snake at a Pen Club Conference in Venice. I turned upon Dovebasket. 'Give me that foul instrument,' I cried in a voice of thunder. 'I confiscate it. And as soon as it is safe to get down I shall conduct you to your Chief of Mission.'

But he only smirked. He was incorrigible, the little blackhead. When later that day I told Polk-Mowbray about the whistle he was beside himself with rage. 'Dovebasket must go,' he said in ringing tones. And duly – these things take an age to arrange – Dovebasket went. He was promoted to the rank of Senior Military Attaché in Delhi. Upwards, old boy. It's always upwards in the service. That is, perhaps, the tragedy of it all.

HIGH BARBARY

What I very much enjoy on the second Saturday of the month (said Antrobus) is the little walk across to the Strand for a haircut and a spiritual revamping *chez* the good Fenner. Everything about the operation is reassuring, soothing. As you know, Fenner himself is clearly a mixture of Old Father Time and Dr Freud. The whole Office has, at one time or another, passed through his purposeful scissors. You know how fanatically faithful to tradition the FO is; well, Fenner is a tradition. Why, last week when Toby Featherblow's wife, Constance, popped number four and the thing was found to be positively covered in hair, it was to Fenner that they rushed to have the features disinterred for the purposes of licensing and registration. Otherwise the registrar might have refused to accept what was, to all intents and purposes, an ape. Yes, you can count on old Fenner. He never flinches before reality.

As for the Emporium – with its potted palms, painted mirrors, its pictures of Eights Week in the nineties, its dominating portrait of Gladstone staring out through (or perhaps round?) a Fenner hairdo – what is one to say? It radiates calm and the soothing smell of bay rum or Fenner's Scalp Syrup and Follicle Food combined. Nor does one overhear any low conversation there – just a few choice anecdotes about the Dutch Royal Family, carefully phrased. Fenner is strict: once I remember that two military attachés were expelled from their stools for trying to exchange betting slips. Fenner's scorn was so withering that one of them cried.

But all this one learns to value truly only when one has served abroad – for not the least of the hazards the poor dip has to face is that of foreign barbary. My dear chap, as you walk in, you can scan the row of seated clients and tell at a glance where some of them have been serving. The singular bottlebrush effect of a Siamese haircut, for example, will take ages to grow out and is quite unmistakable. Fenner will shake his head commiseratingly and say, 'Bangkok, I take it, sir?' The poor chap will sit with trembling lip and nod sadly. 'We will see what can be done to save you, sir,' says Fenner and releases a faintly flocculent blast from a pressurized syringe, which at once brings back the flush of health to the raped scalp. You have experienced it. You will know what I mean.

It varies, too, with every country, as do the habits of the various artists. In Italy your barber is apt to sing – a dangerous habit and excruciating for the tone-deaf; moreover he may add gestures to his little aria of a sudden and lop off an earlobe with a fine air of effortless self-distinction. Personally, I would rather have the stuff grow all the way down my back and into my chair than trust an Italian when overcome with emotion and garlic. I have seen it happen. A cousin of Polk-Mowbray still bears a cropped right ear; indeed, he is lucky to have as much of it left as he has – only a wild swerve prevented its total disappearance. Talk about living dangerously!

In places like Germany, for example, one is lucky to be able to get away without a severed carotid. As for the Balkans, they, too, have their fearsome methods, and I have known cases where people took to beards and shingles rather than face up to reality. Of course, the moment they get leave they fly back to Fenner, who cuts back all the undergrowth and serenely removes whatever may have been picked up by the static electricity. At least that was the excuse that Munnings-Mather gave for all the hairpins and Gramophone needles Fenner found in *his* beard.

As for the French – they leave me speechless, positively beating the air. They will either do you a *style pompier*, piling the muck up on the top of your head and pressure-greasing it until you leave marks on the ceiling of every lift you enter, or else they treat you to a razor cut of such topiary ferocity that you come out feeling sculpted. They cut into the stuff as if it were cheese. No. No. You can have Paris. Let me keep my modest tonsure and my

Short-Back-and-Sides Outlook. The Style Fenner (vintage 1904) is my sort of thing.

Why, in Vulgaria, once, things got so bad that Polk-Mowbray was driven, positively driven, to Take Steps – and you know how much he hated the naked thrust of Action. It was during the Civil War when the country was Communist all the week and Royalist at the weekends. Every Saturday morning the Royalist troops came down from the hills and took the Praesidium; every Monday morning they were driven back with heavy losses. Monday was payday for the Communist forces, Saturday that of the Royalist army. This had a strange effect on the hairdressing business, for during the week you only found heavily nationalized barbers at work, while at the weekend you could borrow the five Royal barbers from the other side. The Communists used an unpretentious pudding-basin cut which had been worked out in terms of the dialectic, lightly driving a harrow across the scalp and then weeding with finger and thumb. They were short of instruments because the Five-Year Plan hadn't started to work due to lack of foreign capital. Anyway, during the week you were in the hands of some horny peasant, while if you waited till Sunday you could get a sort of Viennese pomadour which fanned away into wings at the back like a tail coat and carried sideburns of a corkscrew pattern which once made Polk-Mowbray look so like Elizabeth Barrett Browning that the British Council man, Gool, suggested . . . but that is another story.

Yes, the Balkan barber, conditioned by the hirsute nature of his client, has developed a truly distressing style of action – suited to the nature of the *terrain*, I don't doubt, but nonetheless frightful to those who have been decently brought up. They positively plunge into one's nostrils, hacking and snipping as if they were clearing a path in the jungle; then before one can say 'moustache cup' they crawl into one's ears, remorselessly pruning at what (to judge by the sound) must be something as intractable as a forest of holm oak. I shall spare you. You know.

But I think you had left before Polk-Mowbray entered his Do-It-Yourself phase; the state of Vulgarian barbary must have touched him off. He saw an advertisement for an instrument called, I think, The Gents Super Hair Regulator, which from the brochure appeared to be an ingenious comb and razor blade in one; you trimmed as you combed, so to speak. Nothing simpler, nothing more calculated to please. Polk-Mowbray, deeply moved by the discovery, ordered a dozen, one for each member of the Chancery. He was beside himself with pride and joy. Speaking from a full heart, he said: 'From today our troubles are over. I want each one of you from now on to use his little Regulator and so boycott these heathen barbers of Vulgaria.' Well, I don't know if you know the Regulator? No? Be warned then. It is not a toy for frolicking amateurs. The keenest professional skill is needed to work it. Otherwise, it takes huge lumps out of your hair in the most awkward places, leaving gaunt patches of white scalp glimmering through. By lunchtime on that fatal day, the whole Chancery looked as if it had been mowed down by ringworm or mange. Worse still, De Mandeville contracted a sort of scalp-rot which turned his whole skull green. A sort of deathly verdigris set in. He had to keep his hair in a green baize bag for over a week while Fenner's Follicle Food did its healing work – lucky I had brought a bottle with me. But, of course, the sight nearly drove Polk-Mowbray beserk, especially as at that time the two were at daggers drawn. De Mandeville had sworn to try and drive his chief mad by a sort of verbal Chinese torture. To every remark made to him, he would only reply 'Charmed, – I'm sure,' with a kind of snakelike sibilance. It doesn't sound much, but I assure you that after a few days of endless repetition of this phrase (accompanied by the fearful sight of the green baize bag on his head), Polk-Mowbray was practically beaten to his knees.

But probably the most horrifying instance of mass barbary that I recall was what befell the little party of guileless Finns who submitted themselves to a Vulgarian perm in preparation for the National Lepers' Day Ball. That could not be bettered as an illustration of the Things One Is Up Against in the Service. Five of them, including the Ambassadress, were partially electrocuted owing to a faulty fuse. How is it, I ask myself, that they did not know that the light and power arrangements of Vulgaria were so capricious? Yet, they did not. Polk-Mowbray, who was wooing the Communists, had given the Minister for Interior an electric razor which, whenever it was plugged in, fused the lights of the capital. Something of this order must have happened to the innocent Finns. With their crowning glories tied into those sort of pressurized domes attached to the ceiling by a live wire, they were suddenly aware that everything was turning red-hot and beginning to smoke fearfully; the atmosphere was rapidly beginning to resemble that of a Turkish bath that has got out of control. But the Finns are normally an unemotional race and not much given to fruitless ratiocination. It was not until sparks an inch long began to sprout from their fingers that they began to wonder dimly if all was well. By then it was too late.

They were far too hot to hold. The barbers who manfully tried to disengage them retired hastily with burns and shock. In fact they might have been there to this day, fried to a crisp, had not the Diplomatic Corps been passing at that moment in full *tenue*. We were winding our way across the town to lay a rather limp wreath on the Leper Memorial when we saw the smoke and heard the shrill ululations of the feckless barbers. It was more than lucky, too, that Dovebasket should have a pair of rubberized pliers in his uniform pocket. He darted into the smoke-filled cavern and brought his mechanical genius to bear on the situation, snipping the live wires which attached our poor colleagues to the roof. The Finns rolled moaning to the floor in their golden domes, looking like so much science fiction. 'Give them air,' we all cried shrilly, and willing hands carried them out and laid them in a row upon the pavements. All this had the superficial air of being a mass burial, and I personally believe that had it been anyone but the Finns, that would indeed have been the case. But the Finns can take anything with equanimity. Water was carefully poured over them from plastic buckets. They smoked, they smelled like chops frying, but at last they came to their senses.

We did not see them again until the ball that night which closed Leper Week. My dear chap, you have never imagined such hair. It was positively psychoanalytic. Golden wigs of such hellish, blinding, metallic brilliance. The demon barbers had certainly done their work . . . Ah! But I see that Fenner is free at last. More of this anon.

SAUVE QUI PEUT

We dips (said Antrobus) are brought up to be resourceful, to play almost any part in life, to be equal to any emergency almost – how else could one face all those foreigners? But the only thing for which we are not prepared, old man, is blood.

'Blood?'

Blood!

Mind you, I am thinking of exceptional cases, out-of-the-way incidents; but they are not as rare as one might imagine. Old Gulliver, for example, was invited to an execution in Saigon to which he felt it was his duty to go. It affected him permanently, it damaged his concentration. His head is quite over on one side, he twitches, his ears move about. Unlucky man! I cannot claim an experience as radical as his, but I can speak of one which was almost as bad. Imagine, one fine day we are delivered a perfectly straightforward invitation card on which we read (with ever-widening eyes) the following text or something like it:

His Excellency Hacsmit Bey and Madame Hacsmit Bey joyfully invite you to the Joyful Circumcision of their son Hacsmit Hacsmit Abdul Hacsmit Bey. Morning dress and decorations. Refreshments will be served.

You can imagine the long slow wail that went up in the Chancery when first this intelligence was brought home to us. Circumcision! Joyfully! Refreshments! 'By God, here is a strange lozenge-shaped affair!' cried De Mandeville, and he was right.

Of course, the Embassy in question was a young one, the country it represented still in the grip of mere folklore. But still I mean . . . The obvious thing was to plead indisposition, and this we did as one man. But before we could post off our polite, almost Joyful refusals to these amiable Kurds, Polk-Mowbray

His excellency Hacsmit Bey and Madame Hacsmit Bey joyfully
invite you to the Joyful Circumcision of their son
Hacsmit Hacsmit Abdul Hacsmit Bey.

called a general meeting in Chancery. He was pensive, he was pale and grave, quite the Hamlet. 'I suppose you have all received this,' he said, holding up a pasteboard square on which the dullest eye could descry the sickle and minarets of the Kurdish Arms with the sort of crossed cruets underneath.

'Yes,' we chorused.

'I suppose you have all refused,' went on our Chief, 'and in a way, I am glad. I don't want my Mission to develop a taste for blood . . . these things grow on one. But it does raise rather a problem, for the Kurds are a young, buoyant, up-and-coming little country with a rapidly declining economy, and they are fearfully touchy. It is inconceivable that HMG should not be represented at this affair by *one* of us. Besides, who knows, it might be informal, touching, colourful, even instructive . . . what the devil? But *someone* should be there; we just can't ignore two-legged Kurds in the modern world. The next thing is they will vote against us in UNO. You take my point?

'Well, I have sat up all night worrying about the affair, and (having no taste for blood myself) have arrived at a perfectly democratic solution which I know you will approve and I hope you will respect.'

From behind his back came his left hand holding a packet of straws.

'Whoever draws the shortest straw will represent us,' he cried shrilly. We all paled to the gums but what could we do? It was a command. Closing our eyes, lips moving in prayer, we drew. Well and . . . yes, of course I did. I drew that short straw.

I let out – I could not help it – a rueful exclamation, almost a shout. 'But surely, Sir . . .' I cried. But Polk-Mowbray, his face full of compassion, smote me on the shoulder. 'Antrobus,' he said, 'I could not have wished for anyone more reliable, more circumspect, more jolly unflinching, anyone less likely to faint. I am glad – yes, glad with all my heart that fate should have chosen you. *Courage, mon vieux.*'

This was all very well. I wasn't a bit cockered up by all this praise. My lip trembled, voice faltered. 'Is there no other way?' I cried out in my anguish, gazing from face to stony face. There wasn't it would seem. Polk-Mowbray shook his head with a kind

of sweet sadness, like a Mother Superior demobbing a novice. 'It
is *kismet*, Antrobus,' he said and I felt a sort of coffin-lid close on
me. I squared my shoulders and let my chin fall with a thump
onto my chest. I was a beaten man. I thought of my old widowed
mother in St Abdomen in the Wold – what would she say if she
knew? I thought of many things. 'Well,' I said at last. 'So be it.' I
must say, everyone brightened up, looked awfully relieved.
Moreover, for the next few days I received every mark of
consideration from my colleagues. They spoke to me in Hushed
Voices, Hushed Commiserating Voices, as if I were an invalid;
they tiptoed about for fear of disturbing my reveries. I thought of
a hundred ways out of the affair but none of them seemed
practicable. I went so far as to sit in a draught hoping I would
catch pneumonia; I hinted broadly that I would surrender my
stalls for the Bolshoi to anyone kind enough to replace me – in
vain.

At last the day dawned; there was nothing for it but to climb
into sponge bag and hoist gongs. At last I was ready. The whole
Chancery was lined up to shake my hand and see me off. Polk-
Mowbray had put the Rolls at my disposal, pennant and all. 'I've
told the driver to take a First-Aid Kit with him,' he said hoarsely.
'One never knows in these matters.' You would have thought
that *I* was to be the sacrificial lamb from the way he went on. De
Mandeville pressed his smelling-salts into my hand and said
brokenly, 'Do give little Abdul all our sympathy.' As for
Dovebasket, he pressed his Leica upon me saying 'Try and get a
close-up. The *Sunday Times* colour sup is crying out for
something new and they pay like fiends – I'll split with you. It's
one chance in a million to scoop Tony.' The little blackhead! But I
was too broken to speak. I handed the thing back without a word
and stepping into the car cried faintly, 'To the Kurdish Embassy,
Tobias.'

The Kurds had everything arranged most tastefully, I must
say; lots of jolly decent-looking refreshments laid out in a huge
marquee on the back lawn. Here we dips congregated. I noticed
that most Missions had sent acting vice-consuls smelling for the
most part of brandy and looking pale and strained. Now the
Kurds may be a young nation but they look as crafty as some of

the older. The Mission was dressed in spanking *tenue* but in one corner, presiding over a side-table covered in grisly-looking Stone Age instruments, stood a small group of sinister men clad in horse-blankets of various colours. They had shaven skulls and purple gums and they conversed in a series of dry clicks like Bushmen. Faces which suggested nothing so much as open-cast coal-mining. This, I took it, was the Medical Wing of the Kurdish Embassy – the executioners. But where was the little beardless youth in whose honour all this joyful frolic had been arranged? I went so far as to ask.

'Ah,' cried the Ambassador, 'he will be here in a minute. He is on his way from the airport. He arrived from London this afternoon.' I was a bit puzzled by this, but . . . Kurds have their own way of doing things. 'And think of it!' went on the Head of Mission, clasping his hands. 'Abdul knows nothing of all this. It is a surprise for him, a little surprise. He will be very joyful when he sees . . .' He waved at the group of executioners. Well, I thought to myself, let joy be unconfined, and tried to draw strength from some rather good *rabat lokoum* – Turkish Delight – which I found in a corner. After all, one could close one's eyes, or turn the head; one needn't actually *look*, I told myself.

Luckily my fears were groundless. Imagine our collective surprise when Abdul bounded into the tent to embrace his mother and father: instead of some puling adolescent, we beheld a tough-looking youth of some twenty summers with a handsome moustache and a frank open countenance. This was to be the victim! I must say, his frank open countenance clouded as he took in the import of the business. He showed every sort of unwillingness to enter into the full joyfulness of the occasion. Wouldn't you? Moreover, he was just down from Oxford where he had not only taken a good degree, but had got his boxing blue. His mother and father looked troubled and began to urge, to plead, in Kurdish.

But he respectfully declined, giving every mark of disapprobation. He shook his head violently and his eye flashed. At last his father lost patience and motioned to the thugs in the corner. He was going to force him to enter into the joyfulness of the occasion. But the young man had learned something at Oxford. With a right and left he sent two sprawling; the others climbed on his back. A terrible fracas broke out. Cartwheeling round like a top with the Kurds on his back, Abdul mowed half the Corps down and upset the trestle tables; then, reversing, knocked the tent-pole out and the whole thing collapsed on us in a billowing cloud of coloured stuff. Shouts, yells . . . I lost my topper, but managed to crawl out from under. I tottered to the gate yelling for Tobias. All I got out of the affair was the box of Turkish Delight which I shared round the Chancery. It met with approval and I was the hero of the hour. Compliments? They fairly forked them up to me. Polk-Mowbray was in two minds about the sort of figure I had cut, but after giving it thought he summed the matter up jolly sagely. 'In diplomacy', he said, 'it is so often a case of *sauve qui peut.'*

THE LITTLE AFFAIR IN PARIS

I wonder if I ever told you (said Antrobus) about the little affair in Paris? No? Well, normally I don't care to rake it up, it's too painful. But today I was reminded of it when I filled in my Insurance Medical. O'Toole swam into my mind's eye. My God, you have no idea.

The thing was I was going on leave and made the mistake of asking Polk-Mowbray if there was any little service I could perform for him in the capitals through which I was was to pass. This, as you know, is the mere rhetoric of diplomacy; nobody but a swine would say yes there was. But he did. Fixing me with somewhat watery eyes he said in a dumb pleading tone: 'You could be invaluable to me, Antrobus. Your mature judgement, your winning ways, your paternal touch . . .' All this may have been true as far as it went. 'I have a delinquent nephew called O'Toole,' he went on, 'who is studying medicine in Paris. I fear that something terrible may befall him. He is baroque, quite baroque. His first report says that he is "carrément funeste" whatever that is.' Mowbray's French is somewhat abraded like mine. I mean we can both say 'Cueillez dès aujourd'hui les roses de la vie' with quite a good accent when passing through Customs, but though it creates atmosphere it is not much of a help.

I braced myself and pointed upwind. 'Come, be a pal,' he said. 'All I ask is that you look him up and send me a Confidential Report on him. You may have much in common, who knows? After all, you'll be staying a day or so to cadge a free meal and rub noses with MacSalmon's Mission, won't you? Spare an afternoon for my wandering bairn.'

Put this way it seemed cruel to refuse. I accepted – O woe to

me, yes, I accepted. But the thing troubled me. As I rubbed on
the mint-flavoured aftershave in the mirror of the Orient Express
I looked at myself with affectionate misgivings. So beautiful and
so Put-Upon.

All the omens were against me. I arrived in Paris during one of
those long national holidays which can sometimes last a week.
Nothing was open. No duty car. Even the Mission was locked up
with everyone away. Even the Chargé was away hunting. The
empty shell of the Embassy was in the charge of an illiterate
washerwoman and a Chancery Guard smelling of absinthe. I
had been counting on a sponge, food and lodging with some
junior who would be proud to know me and house me. But more
serious still was my lolly situation. I had hardly any real script on
me and none of the crisp and crackling. I had drawn the usual
vouchers for travel which would have enabled me to refill my
tanks at selected points and leave not a wrack behind. Couldn't
even change travellers' cheques supposing I had any. And here I
was faced with the prospects of a hotel bill as well. What to do? I
pondered as I studied the news bulletin in the Chancery. There
was not a name I knew on the Mission, not a friendly face. And
my God, what low batting averages. I read down the list with
sinking heart. Musgrave, Hoppner, Pratt, Brown . . . all names
now famous to Interpol, but then unknown. They were all
fledglings. It was a newly anointed Mission as far as I could see.
Well, I walked round to try and raise the wind at Goupil, the
Crillon, the Ritz and so on; nowhere could I find a hall porter I
knew. Moreover my train did not leave till Monday. I would
have to spend the week-end in Paris with nothing open but
places of cultural repair like the Louvre – places where I might be
exposed to an unmanning dose of unwanted culture. I knew
how dangerous the French were. Anything but that. I walked
about much struck by the many shops which stocked out-of-the-
way literature and, if flush, might have bought a copy of
Unplanned Paternity, being some hints to mothers by an Unplanned Father; which I believe was written by De Mandeville and
Dovebasket under a pseudonym. But I daren't play fast and
loose with my few francs. I had a glass of Prune Magic in a bistro
and reflected on my lot. Finally I thought of O'Toole. Perhaps he

might help? I unearthed his address. It was within walking distance of where I was. No harm, I thought, could come of passing that way, of conferring a timely nod, a cheerful word on O'Toole. I found the place quite easily, but it was fearfully sinister, and there was a woman in a sort of box, who watched me carefully. She jumped when I mentioned the name and produced a bloodstained cleaver from under her apron. She asked me to give him a message but I didn't manage to get its import. Yet it sounded menacing. She punctuated with the cleaver. I raised my bowler and pressed on up the motheaten staircase to number thirteen. The bell being out of order I rapped with my gamp. There was a pause. Then suddenly everything happened as if in a film. The door flew open, something grabbed me by the necktie, dragged me within and shoved me up against a wall. The door shut behind me with a bang, and a knife was pressed into my tie. I was in the presence of O'Toole. 'One word and I spit you,' he hissed. I was far from uttering a word. I was stunned. He tugged me into a sort of studio and threw me on a couch where I rolled all over my bowler. 'You have come from Them', he said, 'to spy on me. I told my uncle that the next one would suffer. And you're him.' Ignoring his grammar I tried to adopt an ingratiating, a fragrant manner. It was no go. I was up against something beyond me. O'Toole looked like Dylan Thomas after a week on the tiles. Muffler and pork pie hat and all. He looked the hard core of Something. Clearly the soft answer would not suit. Moreover he smelt of plum brandy. He was beside himself. 'Here I am beside myself with troubles and that manumitted mooncalf sends people to spy on me.' His underlip trembled. Clearly the chap was hard pressed. I retrieved my bowler and cleared what was left of my throat. 'Listen O'Toole,' I said. 'Calm your nerves and expose your case to me. Perhaps I can help.' He gave a cry at this and advanced on me with knife raised. 'Perhaps you can,' he said. 'Turn out your pockets.' I'm afraid there was no abiding joy to be drawn from my wallet. Not content in spite of my honest look, he went through my pockets with a practised hand. No, this miserable sum was all I possessed. He walked up and down in a frenzy stabbing at the air. 'What's the problem, O'Toole?' I asked, and something feline and caressing in my tone must have touched a chord for he gave a strangled sob and said: 'My rent is overdue and they are going to take Miriam away. They are distraining on me this evening.' French bailiffs with heavy sideboards were on their way to do away with Polk-Mowbray's bairn. It was sad to see one so young so overwrought. 'But they won't get her,' he hissed. 'I'd rather die.' Gradually I brought myself to bear on the situation, to clarify it; some of what I tell you I only learned subsequently, of course. But for the nonce this reference to his paramour (it would take a Latin to distrain on a girl) nonplussed me. 'Who and where is Miriam?' I asked looking round this gutted building. He pointed the tip of his awfully cutty knife – I can still show you the nick in my shirt where he pressed it home. The electric light had been cut off and the gloom was heavy; but in one corner of the room stood a sort of mummy case. He pointed wildly. 'She's worth two hundred and fifty pounds,' he said. 'Moreover she is my aunt.' Upon my word the damned thing was an articulated skeleton, the sort of thing medical men use to frighten each other on rag day. It was complete. I mean down to the toe. It sagged from a hook in its neck; when you got closer it gave a queer sort of smile. I shuddered. But always loth to abandon a train of reasoning I asked O'Toole to exfoliate a bit, to expand, to explain. Well he had been brought up by a family of sawbones in Dublin who were devoted to the principles of the French Revolution. They had insisted that he study in Paris; Miriam, his aunt, had given her body to science for the honour of the family. It was their only heirloom. Apart from her they owned nothing. But magnanimously they gave it to him on his departure telling him, one supposes, to try and live up to it: and if not to flog it. Now it was going to be distrained upon. The more you see of life the less real it gets . . . The fellow may have been a dastard but I could not help feeling a twinge of sympathy. He was feeling the draught. By skilful questioning I found out the rest. Apparently they could not distrain on him, only on his property; he had managed to get most of his clothes away by walking up and down the stairs in three or four suits at a time and stripping them off in the gents at the local bistro where his friend Coco kept an eye on them. 'But if I tried to carry a bag down the concierge would be on me with that bloody cleaver. I shall have to leave my bags. But what about Miriam?' I could see no way round the affair. Then I saw his eyes narrow; he looked at me in rather a Pointed Way as if he were about to ask for a slice. 'Why do you gaze on me like that?' I cried. I felt some ghastly notion coming over him. Nor was I wrong. 'I have it,' he cried waving his knife with renewed menace. 'You say you've come to help me; well, so you shall.' He opened the window and pointed into the street. 'You will stand down there and I will lower Miriam to you,' he said. 'But if there is so much as a greenstick fracture on her when I get down your fate is sealed.' I tried to remonstrate. After all, I pleaded, I was a British subject, a CMG, a Rotarian and a well-known handbells player. Surely he could not expect me to stand about on a Paris street corner with an unclothed aunt in my arms. He did. He poked me again. 'And don't think you can leg it,' he added. 'I can throw this thing. Look!' He whirled round and pinked the kitchen cupboard.

Well it was a very subdued public servant that made his way down that creaking stair, tipping his bowler to the charmless dromedary in the box who still waited for the distraining force before launching an assault on number thirteen. It felt cold in the street. I felt a certain loss of reality coming over me; I mean it didn't seem to be me any more, my intrinsic me, waiting there gazing up to where, swaying slightly in the breeze, the bones of this venerable aunt descended towards me on a piece of stout cord. I took the pass all right. Miriam, rather heavier than you would expect, was safely in arms. 'Now what?' I called anxiously up into the sky. A policeman had appeared down the corner of the street. He stopped dead in his tracks bemused by the spectacle. I felt deeply conscious of the unclothed nature of the specimen and shipped off my light green plastic mack to work on to her arms. The policeman watched this for a while, pale to the gills, and then muttering something about special tastes, turned round and ran back along the avenue blowing his whistle and calling for witnesses. This sort of thing could only happen at Lourdes, he must have said to himself. There was no time to explain and apologize for now O'Toole bounded from the door

like a Michelin advertisement in his last three suits and four
pullovers. 'Run,' he cried, and carried away by panic, I broke
into a palsied gallop. We shared the burden of Miriam, bursting
like a bomb into the bistro. 'Saved,' cried O'Toole. I don't know
whether you have ever been around with a skeleton in a green
plastic mack, old boy. I don't know how to describe the
feeling . . . It's uncanny. Most of the clients in the bistro paled
under their tan, removed their pipes, seemed about to speak,
and then just swallowed. O'Toole plonked Miriam on a bar stool
and called for three tots. Coco, his friend, took the whole thing
quite normally. I believe he thought that Miriam had been
murdered by O'Toole and then put together in an idle moment
for the sake of company on wet Saturday evenings. I don't
know. Anyway a long confab took place about getting a decent
price for her. This of course caused ears to prick up and ribald
comments to form on various lips. Coco was for selling her to the
Clinique des Pieds Sensibles, but once more we were stymied by
this public holiday. It was shut. I was so worked up now that I
drank Miriam's glass off. Along the street there was trouble
starting; fortunately the police had thrown a net around this
house whose inhabitants spent their time cutting up aunts only
to fall upon the distraining party, bailiffs and beadles and
whatnot dressed in opera hats and cloaks. Thank God we were
just clear; the police arrested the distrainers who resisted arrest
violently. Watching them I felt no joy; only misgiving. For there
on the stool, smiling slightly, sat this damned skeleton. We lay
low for hours while Coco gave us drinks and marked them on a
score card. He told us about his political life. He turned out to be
a red hot revolutionary who walked about Paris at night chalking
'Coco est traitre' and 'Français à moi' on the walls. His party had
a resounding name but according to O'Toole only one member,
himself. Eclectic stuff. But time was getting on; I had to take
myself off and said so. 'By God, you are going to stay with me to
the end,' cried O'Toole, 'or by the bones of Polk-Mowbray I'll slit
your FO weasand.' Polk-Mowbray! I thought of him with such
distaste at that moment. Here I was penniless and trapped by
this aunt-fixated and fuliginous fool.

Coco tried to cheer us up with a song – and he had a fine set of pipes – but I was in no mood for joy. O'Toole thought deeply. Then he said he had it. There was one person who would pay him a decent price for Miriam, a chap called Raoul. But Raoul lived some way outside Paris. We would have to borrow some money somehow. He would pawn a couple of suits with Coco for the journey. 'I don't want to go on any journey,' I wailed. 'Silence Anchovy,' he thundered. 'We are in this thing to the death now.' It was what I very much feared; but I felt weak and defenceless. Miriam had sort of moulded me to her bony will. I won't describe our stately progress across Paris – I'm saving it for the second volume of my memoirs. O'Toole was now under the influence and disposed to be lighthearted to the point of coarseness. But have you ever turned round in a bus queue and seen a skeleton in a plastic mack at your elbow? We spread dismay wherever we went. On the top of a bus he sat Miriam in the seats reserved for the Mutilés de La Guerre and refused to buy a ticket, saying that Miriam had fallen on the Marne. The ticket collector's face worked, his moustache swivelled through 365 degrees but what could he say? How could he prove anything? Several times we lost our way. Once I had to stand alone holding Miriam while O'Toole visited one of those tin shelters where you can see the customers' legs underneath. I was standing on the steps of St Sulpice when another policeman came up to make conversation; did he fear a riot? Did he suspect a crime? I shall never know. He tried to address me, very civilly I mean, and pointed at Miriam. 'C'est la plume de ma tante,' I tried to explain, 'Mademoiselle Miriam.' He said 'Tiens' and raised his shako. But I was so overcome by this effort to explain, and by O'Toole's prolonged absence, that I rushed into the church and hid in a side-chapel. I had hardly started the Lord's Prayer with Miriam kneeling beside me when a verger, white to the lips, came up and hissed at me. 'Get that thing out of here, you are frightening the customers,' was clearly the import of his remarks. Foiled in my intercession with the All-Highest I retreated to the steps and once more met up with O'Toole. Another bus-ride followed, and yet another. I began to feel that everyone in the city must now have seen us with our strange companion. Some thought we were advertising orthopaedic devices. Others that we were Burke and Hare, grave-robbers on a spree. The most charitable felt that we were enjoying a rather unhealthy drollery on our way to the boneyard.

From time to time I half awoke from my tranced state and prayed aloud. But Miriam only smiled. Never have I felt so much the centre of attention. But worse was to follow. We arrived deep in the countryside at a place which sounded like St Abdomen La Boue. We dragged Miriam across a churchyard watched by the furtive peasantry huddled behind trees in copses. We sounded a bell, a door opened and there was Raoul, beret on head and pipe in mouth; we thought we were safe especially as he was overjoyed to see Miriam and agreed on the spot to find her a good home. In fact he waltzed round the room with her in a paroxysm of delight. Then he stopped and his face clouded. Apparently he also was in some kind of trouble. He had fallen foul of the local parson and been denounced from the St Abdomen pulpit on suspicion of practising black magic; the thing was he was trying to grow salads in his garden by the Rudolf Steiner bio-organic method. I am not clear about it but I gathered that in order to get the things to push one had to catch them at full moon, and walk round them reciting mystic runes and playing on a pipe. Enough to cause the darkest suspicions, I'll allow. In fact things had become so hot that he was thinking of shutting up the house and returning to Paris. While he was explaining all this the phone rang. He answered it and jumped a foot in the air. 'They are on their way to arrest me. Someone has told the police that they saw people dragging bodies out of the graveyard next door and bringing them in here. There is no time to lose.' I clutched my umbrella until my knuckles turned white. What new horrors lay in store for us? Outside a sullen church bell began to beat; one could hear the muttering crowd; some stones pelted against the front gate. We sat staring at each other unnerved. Then afar off across the countryside one heard the yapping of a police car racing towards us. 'Quick,' cried Raoul. 'We must escape.' Once again I was seized with vertigo. I cannot remember clearly what happened – how we found ourselves in Raoul's little car, all of us. I sat in the back with Miriam on my knee. As we roared out of the gate in a rain of clods a demoniac scream went up from a thousand throats. Their worst suspicions had been confirmed. A scream of pure horror. Surely a bit exaggerated, but then the untutored peasantry are like that. After all, I was still quite tidily dressed and wearing my bowler. There was no need to imagine that . . .

Across country we went like the wind followed by a couple of black cars full of moustaches. They were gaining on us. 'Faster,' cried O'Toole, and Raoul pressed down until the thing was level with the floorboards. We were cornering much too fast to judge by the scraping noise. Nor could this speed be maintained. We came round a corner and were confronted by a locked level crossing. It was too late to brake. Raoul made a majestic attempt to leap the obstacle; we careered off to one side, through a field and then went smack into the heart of a haystack. I think I must have lost consciousness; all was smoke, darkness and tickle. But when at last I was disinterred I felt a great sense of relief for Miriam was no more. She had been dashed into a thousand fragments. So indeed had we all. The gallant constabulary disinterred us, placed us on ladders and took us back to the ambulance. The next thing was I woke up in the next bed to O'Toole in the local hospital at Moisson. I ached all over but nothing was broken. My nose was blue – this part here. It was a relatively lucky escape. As I lay in a half trance I heard two medical men arguing about our case and the treatment thereof. O'Toole was shamming dead but listening carefully. One voice said, 'I disagree with you, Armand. The Cordon Rouge is powerful enough in a case like this.' The other voice shook its head and said: 'In my opinion only the Imperial will answer.' A frail tremor of joy fluttered in my breast. I blessed a medical profession enlightened enough to prescribe vintage champagne in such cases; it is good for shock, good for bruises, good for everything. Moreover Imperial Tokay, Mumm's Cordon Rouge . . . I didn't really care which. The voices died away and we were alone again. I chuckled and leaned over to O'Toole. 'Did you hear that?' I said. 'We are going to get a champers treatment. Isn't it bully?' But he was bright green, his lips moved in prayer. 'Anchovy,' he said at last, 'you know not what you are saying. Your blithe innocence cuts me to the heart. *The Imperial*

and the Cordon Rouge are the largest suppositories known to science.'
My God! I had forgotten the obsession of the French medical
man with the homely suppos. It is prescribed for everything
from coated tongue to tertiary gangrene. I don't wish to argue its
merits or demerits as a treatment. I have no doubt that in many a
difficult case it works. *But it is prescribed for everything.* There is no
way round it. There I was at the mercy of men with these weird
proclivities. How would I ever face The Office again? A cry burst
from my lips. 'Never!' I meant it. I was seized by a sort of frenzy.
In a moment I had stripped off my bandages, and vaulted out of
my nightshirt into my trousers. Bowler and umbrella were on
the end of the bed. 'Goodbye O'Toole,' I cried in the voice of a
lion and with one bound was at the door. I passed the nurse on
the stairs. She was carrying a sort of bazooka on a tray. I think
she only caught sight of a flash of white as I streaked past her out
into the surrounding countryside. The emergency brought out
all that was most resourceful in Antrobus. I thumbed a ride on a
van into Paris and made my way back to the Embassy
determined to sleep on the doorstep if necessary. But by a stroke
of good luck Glamis Tadpole had come back and was now
receiving. All my troubles were at an end. I accepted a glass of
Scotch and relaxed in the armchair while he made pleasant
conversation. 'I must say,' he said, 'you look very relaxed. You
must have had a jolly week-end.'

Little did he know. Sometimes in my dreams Miriam returns
to visit me; but she has begun to fade. Only now I have got into
the habit of by-passing Paris on my journeys. A man of my age
and in my position of trust can't be too careful, can he?

WHAT-HO ON THE RIALTO!

In the Old Days (said Antrobus) before Time Was – I think it was the year that Mrs Gaskell won the Nobel for England – diplomacy was a quiet and restful trade carried on in soothing inanity among a hundred shady legations and embassies all over the globe. It was hardly more taxing than Divinity for a Scotchman. A fond bland light shone from the old dip's eyes – and why not? Minted at Eton, moulded by Balliol, and mellowed to the sunset tone of old brick by a Grand Tour, the fellow was in clover, and he knew it. Handpicked, packaged, dusted over lightly with male hormone, he was delivered to his post without a bally scratch. Then he had pride: he shaved with nothing but Yardley and scented his beard with Imperial Saddle. Look at the change now: fellows dashed over with cheap and perhaps combustible shaving lotions and industrial talc. Moreover, something else has happened; how has your modern dip acquired his present pinched and furtive look? I will tell you.

It came with The Fall. One day the slumbering dragon in the heart of Personnel awoke and roared: 'Let Woman be given high office.' Woman, dear God! It was the end, old man, and we knew it. We paled to the nape. Our ears went back and stayed pressed close to the head. Urgent confabs took place all over the Office on the intercoms. A hundred voices rose in protest, a hundred plans were made to scotch the idea. Some even spoke of assassination for Gavin Pyecraft who had hatched this grisly scheme. He had always been unbalanced (grammar school). A sort of mystic. He liked custard poured over his prunes. But despite all our efforts the idea caught on and spread. The rot set in abroad as well. It travelled like the Spanish flu. First vice-consuls (a suitable enough title) then Information Girls and finally Female Ambassadors.

All of which brings me to the particular event with which I hope to illustrate my general contention. The French sent in a woman Ambassador to Vulgaria in the form of a handsome, slightly moustached young widow called Mole with a parlous amount of frou-frou and a deadly languid voice which lifted one slightly in one's shoes. The Mission, of course, reeled under the blow, but what could they do? You could hear throats being cleared as she passed. She Walked in Beauty, old Man, Like the Night, to quote someone who ought to have known; easily, lightly, as if on ball-bearings. It made conference difficult to begin with. She had such a lot of different hats; and the way, just the way, she accepted an Aide-Mémoire from the trembling hand of a Head of Chancery made him burn like a volcano.

All might have gone well – but how *could* it? – had not fate at that moment sent in Bonzo di Porco as Italian Head of Chancery. Bonzo was born to be De Mandeville's rival. You never met Bonzo, did you? Well, all technicalities aside, and absolutely without prejudice, he was a fitful little *numéro* indeed. He claimed to be several types of prince and count; his underclothes were spattered with crowns; he drove a cream Hispano-Suiza twice the size of De Mandeville's Rolls. *His* chauffeur was much larger too, and dressed like Robin Hood. Well! You can understand De Mandeville feeling put down. Of course, both men were well-bred in a nervous, mediocre sort of way and it is possible that the iron laws of the Service might have prevented an open breach – had it not been for The Woman.

She flattered Bonzo, making him show off his talents where someone more intelligent might have persuaded him to leave them in the napkin. He played, for example, the flute better, louder, than De Mandeville. His pout was professional, his puff serene and not wavery like that of his rival. Apart from this, he played a blazing game of Shuttlecock. He had actually once had leprosy . . . Oh, I know. You could go on about Bonzo's qualities for ever. But they just made De Mandeville bite his nails down to the quick and *kick* his chauffeur. At Oxford Bonzo had got a first in Lampshade Making while poor De M. had to be content with a mouldy Third in Comparative Lipsticks.

The first round opened with a bit of a mild vapouring and vaunting on quite a high intellectual plane – again because of You Know Who. Where you have French people, you find culture creeping in. (Why, she had the nerve to ask *me* one day 'are you fond of Racine?' to which I riposted instantly: 'I never bet on horses, Madam.')

Well, Bonzo gave it out that he was the only prince in Christendom with a special dispensation enabling him, if he wished, to ride a horse into Milan Cathedral. But he didn't wish, he added modestly. Fifteen–love. Now De Mandeville announced that he had a chit from the A. of C. enabling him to enter the Pump Room in Bath on hands and knees, should he so wish. Fifteen –all. As for the lady, she went on enmeshing them with her veni vidi vici. She had an indelible habit of tapping you on the lips with her closed fan which won all hearts. People queued to be tapped, but none more ardently than Bonzo and his rival. You should have seen them putting up their little faces – like a couple of rudimentary Chinese geese. Their encounters at her table, albeit couched in a highly allusive intellectual vein, were getting more and more acrimonious. De Mandeville started a war of quotations which harassed his enemy on the flank until Dovebasket pinched his 'Dictionary of' and sold it to Bonzo privately. De Mandeville said – just as an example – that when Shakespeare wrote the words 'more honoured in the breech than the observance' he was thinking of someone like Bonzo. Thirty-forty. Bonzo replied that the poet Wordsworth wrote:

> A varlet by the river's brim
> A simple varlet was to him

when he was clearly thinking of somebody of the De Mandeville Stamp. Deuce.

It could only end one way. One evening, at a cultural soirée in the Froggish Embassy, they came to an open breech as to who should turn over the lady's music. Pull followed pull, push, push. I ask you to believe me when I say there was a mild scuffle. They pulled each other's ties and stamped. The lady fainted, and leaving her like a fallen ninepin, they stormed out into the night in different directions.

One evening, at a cultural soirée in the Froggish Embassy, they
came to an open breech as to who should turn over the lady's music.

At this point De Mandeville said it couldn't go on. De Mandeville said that the world wasn't big enough for him and Bonzo too – one of them would have to go. De Mandeville referred darkly to duelling pistols, but when Dovebasket produced some, he showed a marked disinclination to touch them. Dovebasket worked with all the ferocious power of his evil genius to get these two frantic men up to the popping crease but they wouldn't bat, it seems. Dovebasket sent both of them repeated challenges in each other's names trying to help the situation to mature fruitfully. But no. Somehow they managed . . . but as a matter of fact, I mean, what could one visualize as being suitable weapons for single combat – syringes?

But Dovebasket wasn't finished yet; he had recently seen an Italian opera and had been much struck by the presence throughout the action of some fellows of gamesome look on the stage: they appeared to have no stable employment, to be of no fixed abode, and to be loitering with intent. What they did do, occasionally, was to slit a throat on request for a derisory sum – the price of a second helping. Their clients were all in high places and hoping to inherit from the people whose weazands had been slit by this little band of chaps – these 'bravos' for that is the word. Dovebasket was charmed by a profession so . . . how would you put it? It differs slightly from diplomacy, anyway. He persuaded De Mandeville that the bravo was by no means extinct and that Bonzo had several of them suborned in his Embassy. He, De Mandeville, should watch out. He did much the same to Bonzo, and for a while they neither of them dared to go out after dark. From this it was but a step to persuade both men to pay a large sum to a couple of Chancery Guards to be their bodyguards. These they armed to the teeth with an airpistol. Dovebasket got a percentage. But he was not finished yet.

Came the fateful fancy-dress ball given by the unsuspecting Norwegians: in the Chancery we groaned as we noticed the stipulations about dress: 'Masked and about to spend an evening of Carnival in the sixteenth century'. Everyone groaned: this meant we should all have to borrow costumes once more from the wardrobe of the National Opera. Venice! De Mandeville knitted harder than ever as he wondered whether perhaps he might not be poled into the Embassy lying down in a gondola in a cloak? He was toying with this idea and explaining its virtues to me – Bonzo would never think up anything like that – when Rosencrantz, I mean Dovebasket, came sidling in to whisper in his ear. What he said parched him a bit. Apparently Bonzo was going to press things to their limit: his bravos had orders to get De Mandeville during the masked ball. 'I certainly should not stir without your own bravos,' said Dovebasket.

'But it's in costume!'

'Then they too will be costumed and armed. I should see that they have a sword and buckler each at least – if not a reversible bassinet too.'

'Why reversible?'

'To catch the blood in.'

'I see.'

De Mandeville looked somewhat pale. Dovebasket slipped away to telephone to Bonzo in much the same terms and made his flesh creep at the thought that De Mandeville and his two bravos had decided to eliminate him. Which would get who first . . . that was the problem, if you understand me. How?

Well then, let us turn to that fatal evening. You must picture us – a rather listless mob of strangely shaped men clad in brilliant but somewhat grubby reminiscences of Venice. Enormous trousers which our robust forefathers used I think to term 'gallygaskins': two hundred bolts of bombazine to every tuck. Then enamelled codpieces with dependent froggings and perhaps a calico fascinator or two. Moreover, we were all masked and wore upon our heads those strange hats which are apparently given away with every free D. Litt at Oxford. Lampshades, old man, snuffers, dreaming abat-jours at Oxenford.

Well, there we all were, after some insipid chambermusic, when the wrath of the Lord was unleashed. Dovebasket suddenly, with no warning, unsheathed a serviceable-looking cutlass, gave a fearful growl like a mastiff, and launched a terrific slash at . . . I blush to say it . . . his innocent white-haired old Ambassador. 'Answer for your sins, Mowbray,' he yelled as he

drove the weapon home. Well, not quite home. In matters of
self-interest, Polk-Mowbray could show a turn of speed. It was
the public interest which rendered him lethargic. He had been
having a delicious evening, full of clean fun, and admired his
costume which made him feel like the Bashaw of Hendon. Now
suddenly this apparent maniac was on him nip and tuck. It is to
his credit that his jump took him almost to the mantelpiece.
Dovebasket wheeled about and addressed himself to the
American Minister, who gave a wail of mortal terror and
manfully unsheathed his own sword and fended off the lunatic,
being driven swiftly back to the garden balustrade over which he
fell into a flowerbed. He had hardly time to ask what in the name
of flaming Jesus was going forward before disappearing into the
void. Everyone was startled and drew their swords. Some
started as a joke, but no sooner were they poked than they
turned nasty. The women screamed and got under the piano.
Pretty soon a general mêlée started and I decided that it was time
for me to seek the only place of shelter on such evenings – the
curtains. It is perhaps the Polonius in me, and I am not
unmindful of his fate; nevertheless . . . By now there was a
dreadful noise of cold steel on steel, like some fearful knife-
grinders' agape. It is a mercy no one was actually killed. Perhaps
the swords were from 'property' or perhaps it is just that dip
skins are inordinately thick. Anyway, apart from the Chaplain
who was transfixed to the grand piano through his gaskins, no
harm was done; people began to unmask and the panic to die
down. Only, in the centre of the room, six figures still clashed
away; I took it that they were Bonzo and De Mandeville with
their respective bravos. This looked much more spirited and
even promising. Pretty soon, one felt, there would be some
figures lying Strangely Still upon the carpet, and one of them,
Pray God, would be De Mandeville. But no. Heaven intervened
in the shape of the butler, Drage, Bible in hand. With his
experienced eye he took in the scene; with his experienced hand
he did the only thing. He stooped and pulled the carpets and the
contestants, reeling, fell – their hats rolling off, their masks
slipping. A singular sight was revealed. Bonzo had been fighting
his own bravos. So had De Mandeville. It was a miracle that

neither had been punctured. While they were still sitting on the floor comes this female Ambassador and in a voice of thunder, I mean the voice of a thrush, shouts, no, I mean warbles: 'I order you to desist.' She tapped their lips and they were speechless. She ordered them to make it up and with a groan they fell into each other's arms. So ended this fearful ordeal.

Well, from then on things went a bit better and both men won their service medals; as for the lady, she afterwards went to Russia, they say, taking her culture with her, and there had quite a success. She liked the place, the people, and the system so much that she had herself nationalized and married a collective farm. Presumably there she is today. But in my view, old man, woman's place has always been on the farm.

ALL TO SCALE

The thing was (said Antrobus) that Professor Regulus was sent to us by Protocol as the Embassy sawbones. He was a nice compact little man with *pince-nez* and a fine reputation with the full syringe. Moreover he was pro-British, unhealthily so as it turned out. He kept closely in touch with home affairs, borrowed my *Times* and so on; and this was how he got to learn of the PM's gout. I expect you remember the time when it got so bad there was talk of a Day of National Temperance and Prayer, a special service in Paul's and so on. Well Regulus took it much to heart and one Monday he tapered up to the Mission holding a bottle of something called The Regulus Tincture – his own invention he said. He set it down on my desk and gave me a brief insight into gout. It was, he said, just a sort of scale which collected on the big toe like the scale in a kettle. His Tincture, which was made of a mixture of arrowroot and henbane on a molasses base and macerated with borage – his Tincture simply dissolved the scale and liberated the shank. It had, I must say, a funny sort of colour; when you shook the bottle it kind of seethed. I took it in to show Polk-Mowbray who was very touched by this proof of anglophile concern. 'By Gad,' he said, 'we shall pack it off to the PM. Perhaps there's enough for the whole front bench. What a fine fellow Regulus is. Stap me but I'll put him up for a gong.' I went down to have the bottle wrapped up and bagged; on the way I met Dovebasket, who was always keen on science, and dazzled him a little with my grasp of things medical. 'Just like scale?' he said with curiosity. 'I think we ought to try a drop or two.' I did not quite understand, but followed him into the garden where his new sports car stood. Before I could bring to bear he had tipped a cupful of the Tincture into the radiator. Talk about scale! There was a tinkle and a rain of scale fell out on the gravel. Smoke rose from the radiator tap. 'Stand back,' I cried. It was heating up. There was a snap . . . By Goodness this was some mixture. 'We ought to try some on Drage,' he said moodily, but I did not want to experiment any further. The stuff was good on scale and that's as far as I wanted to go. I didn't wish to probe any further. I hoped it would bring great and lasting benefit to the nation and the party. I took the bottle down to bag room and sped it off.

Some time passed before we heard anything from London; then came a somewhat sullen response saying that the PM had tried it on one of his foodtasters who had gone berserk and run the length of Ealing Broadway shouting 'Thrope for Labour' – his name. The bottle was returned to us with this disquieting information and with the distinct order from the FO to try it out in the Mission and to report on its properties to the Foreign Secretary. Well, I mean to say: I have never been backward when it comes to self-sacrifice but I did not fancy a dessert-spoonful of this stuff after what I had seen it do to Dovebasket's radiator. Besides the only one of us who was honestly scaly was Polk-Mowbray; he had in fact been rather proud of his gout and inclined to boast about it. Here was his chance, you would have said; but no he did not seem to see it in this light. He sat, a somewhat pale individual in his heather mixture, and glared at the bottle on his desk. 'I don't want to be cured of my gout,' he wailed. 'It's the one proof I have that the blood of the fourteenth earl runs, though in somewhat tributary fashion, through my veins.'

We debated the whole matter at length; the FS's order could not be lightly set aside. Someone would have to report. Finally it was decided to try a control experiment on Drage and see how that went. It was not hard, for Drage used to drink an occasional glass of Gaskin's Imperial Ginger Wine; in fact he was allowed whenever we had a Royal Toast with lowered lights etc. to join us in pledging his sovereign with a sip of the cordial muck. What easier than to insert a normal dose of the Tincture into his bottle? We watched with intense scientific curiosity that night as Polk-Mowbray dowsed the glims and raised his glass while Drage padded across the room to his cordial and poured out a medium-sized firkin of the stuff.

It was impressive, even riveting. The fellow appeared to have swigged off a glass full of molten lead. A high screech rang out, and he seized his own ears as if he were about to pull them off. Then he started to shadow box, upsetting the candles, and incidentally setting himself alight. What with trying to restrain and comfort him and at the same time to beat out his burning waistcoat there was a vast amount of confusion. What an impartial observer would have made of the scene I know not. Drage vaulted on to the window-sill and still screeching raced off into the night like a hare, tearing off burning articles of clothing as he ran. He left us, a sobered group of palish persons contemplating the ruins of the dinner and the fearful effects of the Regulus syndrome. 'By God, what cracking stuff,' said Polk-Mowbray. 'I suppose we'd better tell the police to look out for a flaming butler what?' It was a pity really that the PM hadn't had the benefits of this terrific tonic; he might have galvanized the party on it. But our hearts were heavy, for we loved Drage; and there he was galloping across Vulgaria tracing a comet's path. It was three days before the police found him and brought him back to us on a stretcher looking pale but sentient. He told us that the stuff had *turned him into a werewolf* for twenty-four hours. At this Polk-Mowbray, always capricious, suddenly flew into a temper with Regulus. 'Imagine it,' he cried, 'this man solemnly urging on us stuff capable of turning a Head of Mission into a werewolf, however harmless. By Gad it is not in nature. It might have happened to me anywhere. Suppose I had bitten Has-drubal or some other member of the Central Committee? I must speak to Regulus and sharply.'

But the next morning the OBE which Polk-Mowbray had secured for Regulus came through on the wire. 'It's a bitter pill to swallow,' he said. 'Just as I was about to berate the man here comes this blasted decoration; what possessed me to do it?' How was I to know what possessed him? One could only say that at the best of times Polk-Mowbray's sense of cause and effect was jolly sketchy. 'And the final annoyance,' he said, giving rein to his mean side 'is that we'll have to toast him in champagne and it's gone up a pound a case.' By custom Heads of Mission paid for this out of their own *frais*. It was Dovebasket who suggested that we should touch up the Professor's drinks with the Tincture as a sort of revenge, and on the purely superficial plane the idea had charm. But the risks were great. We could not have werewolves cantering about the Embassy grounds yelling 'Thrope for Labour' in Vulgarian and perhaps dishing out septic bites. No. We debated the matter from every angle but finally we agreed that Regulus should drink of the true the blushful in a state of nature: if there were any beaded bubbles winking at the brim it wouldn't be the Tincture. So grave was the danger, however, that I did not dare to leave the bottle lying about. Not with people like Dovebasket and De Mandeville in the Mission. So we trotted solemnly out on the lawn in the presence of each other and there I uncorked and poured away the Tincture. Everything smoked and turned blue for a minute. Then we walked back through the clouds to the buttery for a Bovril. If ever you revisit the Vulgarian Mission you will see that there is a huge circle burnt in the lawn; despite every effort nothing has ever managed to grow in that place. Some Tincture, what?

If you were to surmise (said Antrobus) that all our problems in the Vulgarian Mission were political ones you would be Gravely In Error. The dip's life is never as clear cut as the Wars of the Roses; in fact its sheer variety is equalled only by its inanity – as Poincaré once nearly said. Perhaps that is why we enjoy such a range of topics for conversation – no facet of experience has left us unmarked. That is why your hardened dip is not the man to be unnerved merely by the patter of rain on a brushed bowler. He has seen deeply into the secrets of nature. Well, my boy, these reflections – graver than is my wont – have been pooped off by today's *Times* which announces that old Sammy is finishing his memoirs. Poor old Sam – he was once described admiringly by Eisenhower as a supramundane lush. I expect he is going to get his own back in print somehow; he can just read and write – Eton, of course. But it's slow work and it must have taken him years to amount to a book. And then, of course, he's getting on and his career was often dappled with shadow. I mean, he started out with a regulation hip-flask and ended by drinking unrefined embrocation from a hip-bath. Or so they say in the Bag Room where the actual hip-bath may still be viewed for a small *douceur*. No one was really surprised when he took refuge in the Church. For years now we've had vague reports of him stumping round some sodden Suffolk parish clad in a strip of roofing felt. At Xmas time . . . but why go on? The man has suffered; he is trying to atone by a little mild beadling. In the long unheated nights he sits and writes. What does he write? Well may you ask what old Sam is writing. It is not *The Schoolgirls' Wonderbook of Booze and Sex* – no. It is a volume of DIPLOMATIC MEMOIRS. Its title is *Seraglios and Imbroglios* or

. . . old Sammy is finishing his memoirs.

Glimpses Behind the Bead Curtain of Diplomacy by One Who Was There and Suffered For It. Has a sinister sort of ring, no? God knows I hope – everyone hopes – he will be discreet.

My misgivings have increased of late after a talk to Gormley who claims to have spoken to Sam recently on the phone. Apparently Sam said it was all about diplomacy from the religious angle. Now that puzzled me. The only religious chap we had was the chaplain and he left under a cloud, all hushed up. And yet . . . I wonder. There were strange aspects of our lives out there which I suppose one could call religious – if one strained the Official Secrets Act until it creaked. Morris-dancing on the lawn – wouldn't that qualify? With De Mandeville and his chauffeur all cross-gartered and with gipsy earrings. But there was nothing religious about Polk-Mowbray's outburst when he saw them . . .

Then I remember little Carter – if that was the name. Americans are notoriously Romance Prone. He went off to Egypt on leave with the ALEXANDRIA QUARTET under his arm. Next thing we knew, he had become a Moslem – bang! just like that. Gone over to them bodily. He came back from leave looking pale but jaunty in a ghastly sort of way and towing a string of little new black wives. Real ones. 'Durrell's right,' he is alleged to have announced to his Chief with an airy wave. 'Down there almost everything goes.' Well, of course, he went too; but he had brought us a headache. Things like this can be very catching in the Corps. He had Raised a Precedent. Yet technically he was quite within his rights. There was no religious bar in the State Department nor in the FO. They had the devil's own job to post him: there was no excuse – being American he was efficient. Nothing left but to upgrade him and send him to UNO where he would be lost in the dusky spectrum. I met Schwartz their Councillor looking pale and fagged out; I knew why. It was this damned business, all the telegrams flying about.

'It was such a quiet mission,' he wailed, 'before This. What did he want to do it for?' Schwartz played bridge every day of the week and the thing was gumming up his concentration. Through the open window we could see Carter taking his wives for an airing on the Embassy lawn; since they could not speak each other's language, he was playing leap-frog with them. The staff stared down through the windows, their faces working. Schwartz stifled an oath. 'Antrobus,' he said, 'you know and I know that technically speaking there is nothing in the regulations to prevent King Solomon strolling into the State Department and asking for a posting – even if he were to jerk his thumb (here Schwartz jerked his thumb) and say "These ladies here, by the way, are my wife; kindly put her on K rations".' I felt for him. Yes, Carter cost us a great deal of extra legislation. After all, what was to prevent the whole State Department filling up one night with Mormons? Well, the waters closed over little Carter. I was sorry for him. Two of the wives were quite pretty, they said, with well-placed Advantages. But it was useless crying over spilt milk. We reformed our ranks and marched on, ever on.

You see what I mean? Hardly the sort of thing one wants written up by Sam. Besides, this Carter episode touched off a powder-barrel in our own Mission. We were unaware that we were sitting on it. Mind you, I had smelled burning for some time but couldn't locate the site. You remember Drage? Of course you do. Yes, here we are truly in the field of Revealed Religion. All that winter the Visions had been gaining on him, the Voices had been whispering seditious info into his faun-like ears. Also he was at war with Dovebasket – always a dangerous thing, and now doubly so for that human vacuum had just taken a degree in applied electronics. Drage alarmed me, Dovebasket disgusted. I held no brief for either. But things went from Bad to Worse, and the food began to go blazes. The Instant Pudding refused to stand to attention. Dovebasket had fixed the bunsens in the kitchen to such good purpose that Drage virtually found himself supervising nuclear tests with self-raising flour. De Mandeville worked out a Menu for the French Mission Dinner which was too near the bone to raise anything but the hollowest of laughs. It spoke of plovers' eggs in ether and baby rusks marinated in nitric acid. It hinted at cocktails of lemon curd and ammonia with just a touch of machine oil from the crank-case of some abandoned locomotive. Gods! There was even the British Club Sandwich which he diagnosed as consisting of old raffia work with thin slices of thrice-triturated gymnosophist. Drage seemed to have gone dead Continental. And still the Visions pressed on him, thicker and faster. Finally Drage was forced to ask for religious help from the leader of his sect – a Nonconformist preacher called Fly-Fornication Wilkinson. He was a tall spindly man with a goatee and huge goggles. Little comfort, I should have thought, could be derived from his strange allure. But what to do? We could all see that the fellow had a mushroom-shaped psyche. His voice was deep and boomy with an occasional scream like a police whistle on the word 'sin' which made one sit up and metaphorically spurn the gravel with one's hooves. He moved into Drage's cottage to offer him the occasional winged word. Next thing was Drage asked if he might address us on a Sunday and preach a sermon. The Chaplain was away playing roulette in Nice that week. In matters of religion we are extremely liberal. I could hardly refuse.

The fellow took as his text 'King Solomon in all his glory was not arrayed as one of these.' The hats of the Embassy ladies had apparently caused him grave offence. He pointed at them as he lashed out at us. His words whistled through the side-chapel like grape-shot. De Mandeville paled and began to sob quietly into a cambric handkerchief. To hear him you would have thought the typists' pool was rotten to the core and that Polk-Mowbray was living a life of untrammelled lubricity with a cageful of nightingales. I must say!

Yet for the first time as we listened we all began to feel a kind of sneaking pride in Dovebasket, a warmth about the heart. He had bugged the pulpit. He was going to avenge us – even though his real target had been the unfortunate Drage. Never mind. The Rev. Fly-Fornication was going to receive the charge. I must say, though, he was game: despite every set-back he plunged on with his sermon. Flames leapt from the harmonium when Miss Todger's elfin foot touched the treadles. They were gallantly beaten out with Polk-Mowbray's overcoat. Wilkinson resumed his discourse. Electronic devices buried in the walls now opened up a barrage of jungle music, cowbells, mating cats and so on. Wilkinson tightened his pegs and let his voice soar above it. Then on the wall behind us appeared a giant coloured projection which said 'REPENT YOU DOGS', and then another saying, 'DRAGE, I'VE COME FOR YOU, YOU BASTARD'. This was signed 'Jaweh' in an illiterate schoolchild's hand. It was clearly going to be a battle to the finish, for the undismayed preacher gathered himself together and ploughed on. Dovebasket was looking pale and tense now. Was he going to lose the day? Desperate measures must be taken. He must play his last card. Trembling with excitement, he leaned forward and pressed switch F under the pulpit. Thank God, it worked. A six-pound boxing-glove slid out of the wall with a smart click and dealt the reverend gentleman a massive thump below the left ear. It was the pay-off. He fell out of the crow's nest on to the much-tried front rank of the Mission. His head came dreamily to rest on Polk-Mowbray's knees. The world suddenly looked brighter. I could hear the birds singing in the Embassy shrubbery. Loving hands were there to gather up the pieces, to dispose the body for burial. But Wilkinson still breathed. He was flown home on a stretcher at Crown expense. Moreover, Drage was cured as if by a miracle; at least temporarily. The cooking swung back to good plain home. He still retained Wilkinson's Bible and from time to time would read from it in a voice mossy with gutturals and general tonic sol fa. But the worst was over. Drage had become an ordinary butler again, a human being full of ordinary old-fashioned blood.

I could give you many other examples of what one might call the religious impulse in the Corps; it varied. enormously. I hope Sam takes advantage of some of the more colourful episodes, like when Polk-Mowbray decided to build a Marxist chapel in the Embassy grounds to try and wean everyone from Barren Materialism. It got as far as the drawing-board stage before being shot down. Mercifully, political reasons intervened. For who would consecrate such a structure? The style was a sort of Primrose Hill Wesleyan. I believe John Betjeman was approached, but nothing came of it. The Russian Mission was particularly touchy. Their Chargé was a curious piece of Volga folklore called Damnovich. He had a sort of three-dimensional Marxist smile. He had been eaten into by the dialectic. One day he disappeared from sight and it was strongly rumoured that he had committed hara-kiri in the most original style. He had received a reproof for some minor dereliction of duty and took it so much to heart that he made the honourable amend by having himself marked TOP SECRET and carried out to the incinerator where he perished along with Confidential Waste. Clever, no? But not half as tortuous as Reggie Subtitle who was determined that his brother was not going to inherit a bean when he died. His will was a masterpiece. He had his embalmed body sent back to the sarcophagus in Coutts's Oxford Street Branch where it still lies in a cellar along with all his furniture and baggage. Nobody can get at it, and without it his brother cannot inherit for Reggie is still posted as Missing – Believed Absent, though all this is years ago now.

One last example – as a warning to junior dips. This happened to me. You know that widowhood is practically a profession in Vulgaria; they were everywhere. Widows. Dressed in rustling black, eyebrows meeting in the middle, heavy moustaches . . . Ninety per cent of the population is widows, or so it seems. Well, we had one of these, or rather, we acquired one. One of the Consular Clerks had perhaps won her in a Christmas raffle? How do I know? Took her instead of the turkey, or even by mistake for it? At all events, she became Mrs Threadneedle. Then her spouse tired of her, so he left his shoes and clothes by the Danube, wrote her a curt farewell on a leaf, and apparently drowned himself; in fact he panted across the frontier and returned to civil life where he is deeply respected in Banbury as an estate agent now. How were we or she to know? We wrote him off and indented for another. Meanwhile, Mrs Thread-needle, justifying her existence, raised a Point of Order. Apparently widows were no longer entitled to bonded drinks and smokes: wives, yes. Not widows. She could not quite understand this and her English was too sketchy to enable us to expose our case to her. It carried no conviction. Moreover, she had somehow been led to believe that when one was short of a British Subject, or when one had mislaid the one in hand, one could simply trot up to the Mission and select another. It was the question of bonded goods that agitated her. She took to coming up and sitting outside the Chancery door and pleading with us as we passed to and fro. Finally she decided, since there was no help for it, to select another spouse for herself so that the interrupted flow of bonded gin and Benson and Hedges might be resumed. Her choice fell upon me. I don't know why. Perhaps it was my open face which seemed to betoken a liberal nature. At any rate, when I passed her she would point a finger at me and cry 'I will 'ave 'im'. It caused a good deal of innocent amusement to all but myself. I was scared stiff. Soon she made grabs at my hand to kiss. The situation had become critical. I could only get to my office now by climbing in at the window; moreover I could only visit my colleagues in the same furtive way. You can imagine how tiring this proved to be. My footsteps ploughed up the flower-beds. My muscles ached. I lost weight. There seemed no way of getting rid of the lady. Once she even came into my office with a priest who blessed me with a sprig of hyssop and covered a despatch with holy water. *She was paying to have me softened up.* I was *in extremis.* Finally I consulted Dovebasket, and it was thanks to his genius that the worst was averted. Taking his advice, I called in Thurston and, clearing my throat, put the matter to him. He was a huge fellow, Chancery Guard.

'Thurston,' I said, 'you have rather a sharp choice before you. You have been drunk on duty for the sixth time running and H.E. has decided to tell the FO. You know what the result will be, don't you?'

He pulled a shaggy forelock and drew on the carpet with his big toe. 'Now', I went on, 'he has left the whole matter to my discretion. I have been pleading with him on your behalf; but it seems to me that your whole trouble is that you are a bachelor. You have too much time on your hands and not enough responsibility. Now if you married, I might reconsider the whole thing; moreover, if you married Mrs Threadneedle I might even upgrade and post you to somewhere where the pay is better.' I let all this sink in a bit. The fellow blenched, as well he might; but I pointed out that married men received splendid allowances and decent houses to live in. 'Go away and debate the matter and let me have your reply not later than this evening.' The firmness of my tone, the sweetness of my voice had a deep effect on him. By that evening he had made his choice: Mrs

Threadneedle would become Mrs Thurston. Imagine my relief. But the strange thing was that the marriage worked: Thurston signed the Pledge and started a new life. When I left, they were both singing in the choir. Say what you like, there must be something in religion.

AUNT NORAH

More than once (said Antrobus) have I seen my Chief shaken, sometimes even brought close to breaking point: but you should have seen his face when intelligence came that his Aunt Norah was heading south towards Vulgaria, leaving a train of carnage behind her in Paris and Rome. It was a cruel thing to happen to him, particularly at his time of life with retirement so near. Yes, he was old by then, a somewhat battered repaint; but this bit of news had him skipping like a stag. In those days he was rumoured to wear Dunlopillo trousers so that he could sit down without bruising his ideas – but this was mere malice on the part of Dovebasket. Aunt Norah now . . . Of a sudden he was sad, bowed; he lowered his undercarriage and trimmed his flaps and cried: 'No.' Once, just like that, 'No.'

I cannot disguise the fact from you that she had gone a little queer in the head with the passage of the years. At first she was mildly eccentric; but what got her turned off clear was that she happened upon some Labour Party pamphlets and was at once captivated by their attitude to sex. I mean about having lots more about and teaching the young and so on; and to have more pictures of Bernard Shaw over the nuptial bed to promote conception. I don't know. I never took a lot of it in myself. Rum stuff I found it, in places downright unmannerly. But that is what Labour stands for they say. Well anyway the Scales Fell from Aunt Norah's eyes when she read Shaw on how to be more all-embracing. Why Shaw I wonder? Nobody came down with powder markings after kissing him did they? Anyway she was converted and decided to promote the good cause by lecturing on sex to the young of foreign nations, starting with the French. Of course the trouble is that you can't illustrate sex for young people as clearly as you can Euclid; the human body has too few acute angles or hypotenuses – or so they tell me. But she did her best. Her huge diagrams looked like a study of the internal measurements of the Grand Pyramid; there were logarithms, isotherms, isobars and heavy pressure belts like a weather forecast. It was impressive. We first heard of traffic jams and cheering crowds and police charges in Paris. The French love intellectual diversions and here she was; she lectured from a table covered in a Union Jack and with a bull terrier called Bernard tied to the leg. She had trained it to growl at various points in her lecture as if to give point to it. Of course all this may have seemed a bit strange to them but then everyone knows that the British have their own way of doing things.

So now Aunt Norah was heading south after tearing Rome apart. 'If storied urn or animated bust' I reflected as I saw my Chief sitting there with bowed head looking as if he had been passed through muslin and was weak and fizzy enough to be sipped through a straw. 'I will hand over the administration of the secret fund for ONE WHOLE WEEK to whoever can think of a way to stop her,' he vowed. Naturally such an idea had great appeal and many were the ideas tried out. De Mandeville, pushed for lolly as always, hit upon a notion that almost worked; he and his chauffeur dressed up as Carmelites and delivered an *aide-mémoire* to the Vulgarian FO protesting about her being allowed in on religious grounds. They were somewhat shaken but stood firm. I think they had glimpsed the suede hacking-shoes underneath the gown. Or perhaps their rosaries looked dubious. Anyway Polk-Mowbray's alarm communicated itself to all of us; we grew morose, edgy, jumpy. After prayers one day De Mandeville struck his head on a beam and was knocked almost insensible; we had to give him the kiss of life with a bicycle pump. When he came to he confessed that he thought he saw Aunt Norah advancing down the drive, hence the jump. Just to show you what a state we were in.

Meanwhile the lady herself was advancing methodically on the capital in a large caravan with 'Hurrah For Sex' on one side, 'Glory to the population bulge' on the other; she pursued her leisurely course across the smiling countryside, stopping in the

little towns to dish out pamphlets and fertility charms and
harangue the multitudes. Of course they couldn't
understand . . . and this is where Dovebasket earned a whole
week of the secret fund. His face ablaze with joy he rushed into
the Chancery shouting: 'I've got it.' We hardly dared to hope by
this time. 'We are fools,' said the youth. 'Aunt Norah knows not
a word of Vulgarian, and who in Vulgaria knows more than the
words "whisky and soda" in our native bow-wow?' We mulled
him over a bit. 'But the riots in Paris and Rome, the march on
Florence – how was this achieved, for clearly she knows neither
French nor Italian?' Dovebasket whinnied. 'Of course. *Interpret-*
ers. We must offer her official interpreters and then suborn them.
While she thinks she is throwing them into a fine lather with her
sex palaver they can be reading strips of Holy Writ like Engels or
Kingsley Martin. In this way we will save our souls.' Polk-
Mowbray had tears in his eyes. 'I believe you have it, my boy,'
he said, fishing out the key and handing it over. 'Now we must
find the translators. Yea, go out Antrobus and find me two little
Vulgarians with flared nostrils and ears too close to the head –
men with the bad breath of taxmen or Marxists.' For once I saw
the road clear. 'Ay, Ay, sir,' I said; and so the whole matter fell
out. Aunt Norah had one of the most successful rallies of her
tour and apart from us all being deafened by Engels all was well.

TAKING THE CONSEQUENCES

I have never (said Antrobus) ceased to preach against paper
games in the leisure hours of the service; either for entertainment of friends or for the killing of time. I have several times
found them a Grave Danger. Nor do I make any exception –
though perhaps the game called 'Consequences' is the worst in
this respect. To my regret Polk-Mowbray could never be got
round to this view; for him no dinner party was complete
without a vapid hand of Pontoon, or Mimsy or Bellweather. All
the pencils were co-opted from Chancery, and all the expensive
minute paper. Down we would sit to wrestle with some inane
problem, feeling like a human fritter; nor could we say him nay.
He *ordered* us to play. It was inhuman, and at times I got so
indignant that I thought I should get circles under my prose or
lose my *vibrato* or both. But Nemesis was waiting in the podgy
person of the Baron Blenkinhoorn, the newly arrived correspondent of the Deutsches Sauerkraut news agency, a powerful
organ of West German opinion. He was a very serious man. His
notepaper had a crown and garter gules. He wore heavy
spectacles and beard brushed back against the wind like Epping
Forest. Whatever you told him he wrote down instantly in a
huge pad and telegraphed to his organ. He lived in the Vulgaria
Hotel and was rumoured to sleep with a pistol under his pillow.
Nor did his seriousness make him endearing, no. Once De
Mandeville persuaded him to publish Polk-Mowbray's obituary
by uttering a false press release. For a man as superstitious as
our Ambassador this gave him quite a fright and the Baron had
some trouble exculpating himself. Quite a huff grew up between
them and it was only rarely that the Baron came into the
Chancery for a brief untainted bit of info. On some such visit he

Baron Blenkinhoorn

must have managed to break down the morale of Dovebasket and make a hireling of him, for his despatches were now full of Inside Info, things he would never have known had he not had an accomplice. For instance that Toby Imhof was even then working on bottled cat's breath to put down mouseholes and had already patented the perfected version of Snarlex, jujube for the tired parent. Where could he have found out I mean? Even the little day-to-day accidents which any normal Embassy has to endure without telling the press. The Baron knew them all and sent them to his organ which duly printed. Nothing appeared to be sacred. It was the year that Angela was sent down for writing Just Married on the back of a police car; Dovebasket, who was mad about her and had been jilted revenged himself by meddling with the taps on the blue room bidet – to such good effect that the wretched girl found herself pinned to the ceiling by a water-jet and had to be got down with ladders. You see what I mean? He finally had us looking over our shoulders. Polk-Mowbray bit his nails to the quick. Particularly as all this stuff was joyfully translated by our German Mission and sent back to the FO. The Foreign Secretary read with popping eye the Baron's account of De Mandeville's dress reform movement which insisted on handbags for men and the wearing of a strange new hat called a Boadicea, with side flaps. The wires began to buzz and we found ourselves issuing Categorical Denials or Studied Evasions in batches of ten. Things could not go on like this. But how to get the Baron out? If only we could get him declared persona non grata by the Vulgarians . . . But his integrity was perfect, he neither smoked nor drank, and women were mere furniture. We ran through a number of schemes, mostly counsels of desperation, like introducing highly trained crabs into his bath. De Mandeville who was white with rage tried to get up a plot to murder him outright by waxing the dance floor to a preternaturally high gloss and inviting the Baron to a ball where Angela, who had agreed to sacrifice herself, was to lead him out for a Waltz and then turn him loose to break his neck. We were foiled. The Baron didn't dance, and of those who did several broke their collar bones and ankles. No, he was a tough nut to crack. We put Scooter, our secret service fellow, on to

The British Ambassador met
Mrs Kruschev
In a lift.
He said: 'Will you be my satellite?'

him, to study his little weaknesses; but he had few, unless you count spending hours and hours alone playing on a portable clavichord.

Meanwhile the Revelations went on; some of them were so extraordinary that Polk-Mowbray nearly went out of his mind. The Foreign Sec. wrote him in prose of a secular tautness, asking him whether or not the following were true: a secret meeting with Mrs Krushchev to negotiate a pact without telling HMG. Another less secret with Pandit Nehru outside a public *cabinet d'aisance* in Bombay. A third with Stalin. A fourth with the Baroness of Monrovia (a dusky Ambassadress) . . . And so on. 'Antrobus,' he cried out, 'somehow this must stop. Simple denials cannot meet the case. Everyone believes the press, nobody believes a dip. This man has set out to lose me my froggings. Think, man, think.' I thought until I throbbed. Then the idea crept over me that recently we had not heard very much of Dovebasket; he had been living a life of strange and rather suspicious demureness. Something Told Me that if he were not directly responsible for those leaks he might at least have a notion about what to do. I went to see him and tried to rouse his manlier feelings by describing the emotions of Polk-Mowbray. He only laughed like a faun and said 'So he has had enough has he? I was wondering when he would break. Yes, I know what to do, but it will take money and time. For a couple of hundred I could suborn Blenkinhoorn.' The price was outrageous of course but we were trapped. 'So you *are* responsible after all,' I blazed at him, white to the tentacles and practically springing a front stud. 'Explain yourself.'

He wouldn't until I'd handed over the money. Dovebasket counted it respectfully and stowed. Then he said: 'Actually, old Blenky is acting in perfect good faith; it's just that he is short on humour and doesn't know how the other half live. His vision is warped. I was just about to send him over another lot of info for tomorrow's organ. But since you ask so nicely I'll desist. Here, have a look. There's no mystery; I've been selling him the fruit of H.E.'s wastepaper basket. He will insist on paper games.'

I saw a clutch of paper Consequences which explained all. The Baron had been working upon texts which must have seemed

mysterious enough to him in all consequence but which were as
clear as daylight to the normal FO mind:

> The British Ambassador met
> Mrs Krushchev
> In a lift.
> He said: "Will you be my satellite?"
> She said "Squeeze me when the lights go out."
> The result was The Warsaw Pact.
> Polk-Mowbray met
> Pandit Nehru
> Outside a public lavatory in Bombay.
> He said: "Never a dull moment."
> N replied: "I would sell you my soul."
> The result was a small inedible. . . .

But why go on? In a flash one could see how the Baron had
been misled. I mounted triumphantly to Mowbray and waved
the papers. I told him how I had saved the day. The money
would have to come from the secret fund of course. He mopped
his brow and thanked me fervently. Yet Dovebasket did not
escape a Grave Reproof. I distinctly heard Polk-Mowbray saying
to him on the phone: 'You can damn well take a hundred lines,
Dovebasket, yes a hundred. And let them be "In future I must
not be such a blasted Borrogrove".'

I thought that rather met the case.

A CORKING EVENING

All day today (said Antrobus) I have been addressing Christmas Cards, an occupation both melancholy and exhilarating; so many of us have gone leaving no address. They have become 'FO BAG ROOM PLEASE FORWARD', so to speak. Some are Far Flung, some less Far Flung, some Flung out altogether like poor Toby. It is a season which sets one wondering where dips go when they die, old man. Do they know that they can't take it with them, or is there perhaps a branch of Coutts in Heaven which will take post-dated cheques? And if they live on as ghosts, what sort of? Is there a diplomatic Limbo – perhaps some subfusc department of UNO where they are condemned perpetually to brood over such recondite subjects as the fishing rights of little tufted Papuans? Ah me! But perhaps it would be more like some twilit registry where a man might yet sit down to a game of coon-can with a personable cipherine . . .

Yes, as I riffled my address book so many forgotten faces drifted across my vision! Who will ever tell their story? Not me. What has become of Monksilver and Blackdimple – those two scheming Jesuits? What of 'Tumbril' Goddard who believed in the Soviet way of life until he tried *kvass*? What of old 'Tourniquet' Mathews, and 'Smegma' Schmidt, the Polish avalanche? If ever the secret history of The Office is written their names will be blazoned abroad. Some have never had their due – like poor little Reggie and Mercy Mucus, the British Council couple. They died in the execution of their duty, eaten by wolves. Despite a falling glass they tried to cross the frozen lake bearing a sackful of Collins' Clear Type Shakespeares; they were heading for some remote and fly-blown khan where their eager clientèle of swineherds waited patiently, eager to ingest all this foreign lore. In vain! In vain!

Then my eye fell upon the name of Dovebasket and forgotten scenes thronged back, one more painful than the next. I remembered, for example, the age of emulation . . . I have often remarked how emulous Heads of Mission can be. That winter it was champagne. Several old European cellars had been up for sale, and those who had not overspent on their *frais* had cried Snap, among them Polk-Mowbray. He was at that time going through a difficult period. He had become much enamoured of young Sabina Braganza, daughter of an Italian colleague; mind you, all this in a perfectly proper and avuncular way. When she announced her engagement, he was so pleased that he decided to throw a party for the event which would both celebrate her beauty and allow him to show off his champagne. Though often misguided, he was a good man at heart. But he had offended Dovebasket. And Dovebasket harboured a Grave Grudge. He decided to touch up, or as he put it to 'excite', Polk-Mowbray's cherished cases of Pommery. With a blowlamp in hand and clad in a steel-welder's casque he prowled the cellars like a figure from Greek tragedy, warming the stuff up and loosening the wire. The result was unforeseen but satisfying from his point of view. The banqueting room was shaken by dull explosions; some of the bottles went off like Mills bombs, others threw out parabolas of foam. I saw Drage holding one of these spouting bottles up with the astonished look of a man whose umbrella has been blown inside out. Worst of all the Braganza child received a black eye from a cork.

The failure of this party and the fury of the parents all but unhinged Polk-Mowbray; he took to locking himself up, talking to himself, even to starving a bit. It got to such a pitch that he even started sleepwalking. One morning Drage saw him in the dim light of dawn walking out of the Embassy and into the road clad in the blue night-shirt he always wore (with royal arms embroidered on it). It was horrifying. There was our Head of Mission crossing the main road in his tasselled bed-cap, hands outstretched, lips moving. Drage sped after him, Bible in hand. He tried to wake him by talking to him, but in vain. He dared not actually shake him for the person of a Plenipotentiary Extraordinary is sacred and can only be touched, pushed or pulled by someone of equal rank. Drage was at his wits' end; he even read bits of the Gospel loudly to his chief, but to no purpose. All he heard was the muttered whisper 'I have come to apologize.'

They were nearly run down by an early-morning tram full of workmen who cheered them. Then, with increased horror Drage saw him turn into the gate of the Italian Mission and start climbing the ivy towards the second floor where the unfortunate Braganza girl slept. Drage held one ankle and yelled for help. Now the situation was only saved by an extraordinary coincidence. De Mandeville had been on a diet that week, and had been limiting himself to a glass of early morning dew which he gathered himself from the Embassy grass. It was he who, glass in hand, heard Drage's yell from across the road. He bounded to the rescue, and less intimidated by Polk-Mowbray's rank than the butler, sacrificed the dew he had gathered by pouring it down his Ambassador's back.

Polk-Mowbray awoke with a start and fell, bringing down most of the trellis with him. There was a moment of Agonizing Reappraisal as the three of them sprawled among the flowerbeds. Then Polk-Mowbray realized where he was though he wotted not quite how. They rushed, they ran, they galloped back to the safety of the Mission. That morning Drage served them an early breakfast in the buttery and Polk-Mowbray swore De Mandeville to secrecy; he also told him that he was putting him up for the Life Saving Medal – a cherished decoration normally only given to people who rescue dogs from wells. 'Furthermore,' he added – for he knew how to do the handsome thing – 'I want to apologize for making you waste your dew. I know it is jolly hard work gathering it.'

'Not at all, Sir, there is plenty more where it came from.' Upon which amiable exchange the incident was closed. Another sherry?

SMOKE, THE EMBASSY CAT

'I think that enough time has elapsed to permit us to talk about it now – you will say that it is not a state secret, but for a while that damned cat practically controlled the FO. It sends shivers up and down my cummerbund when I think of the extent of Polk-Mowbray's dependence on that . . . spirit-control, there is no other word for Smoke. We still don't know where it came from or even whether it was a he or she or an it. Its bearing was too supercilious to encourage questions like these. Mind you, there was nothing particularly otherworldly about the Mission that winter – no visions from Drage, no karmic seizures from the naval attaché who did yoga, nor any poltergeists moving furniture about in the Chancery. Nothing, in fact, to herald a visitation from what the French refer to so airily as the *au delà*. Looking back on it I am sure now that the cat was a visitant from Beyond the Beyond, an emissary of Old Nick himself.'

I noticed that he looked over his shoulder as he said it, and lowered his voice a bit. It was not even lunchtime, and here he was, looking quite pale. 'Tell me about it,' I said, ordering him a drink.

'Very well,' he said, though he still looked a trifle uncertain of the wisdom of such a proceeding. 'But let us order lunch first while I marshal my facts and put them in order.' He spent a moment or two communing with his drink, and then, joining his fingertips with a forensic gesture, took up the tale of Smoke, the Embassy Cat, and the reign of terror which had followed upon her adoption by the Head of Mission – most guileless of men!

'I have nothing against animals,' said Antrobus, resuming his story, 'and nor had any of us. Put us to the question, and you would not find one who was a vivisectionist. It is true that

George Cromwell once cut up a newt to make a love potion, in the hope of seducing Angela – but the newt was already dead. Anyway the potion didn't seem to work for she threw him over. But that is as near to the heart of the animal question as I have ever penetrated. We respected them, we didn't kick them in the street, but we didn't fawn on them specially. So that Smoke was something quite new in our lives; she or he or it had an effect on every member of the Vulgarian Mission.

'I well remember the day she appeared – I was in H.E.'s office, helping correct some estimates. As usual he had been running barefoot through his statistics. We heard noises coming from his golf bag which suggested that a very small second-hand bagpipe was being squeezed. We thought at first that perhaps it was the Vulgarian caddie that he used on the diplomatic links – who happened to be a dwarf. It was the work of a second to up-end the bag and shake the clubs out on to the carpet. With them came an extraordinary little ball of fluff with huge blue eyes and a tail like a comet's. This is what had been responsible for the noise in the depths of the bag. "On my oath, a cat," said H.E., always ready to extend his jovial condescension to another member of the animal kingdom. "How it cries, Antrobus!" Indeed, how it crew! We put it on his desk where it repeated its strange squonking noise. "It is crying for the breast, sir," I said, which rather startled Polk-Mowbray. Yes, that was it! "Perhaps it thinks you are its mother, sir," I continued. He looked confused – he didn't like to be found wanting. "Milk is the answer to that noise, sir," I said, drawing upon a lifetime's cultural instruction. He put out his hand to stroke the animal and received something like a sabre-stroke across his fingers. He used a very bad word which he had learned at Eton, I believe.

'The world, you know, is made up of two vastly different sorts of people. There are those who remain calm and can look a cat in the eye, just exclaiming, if necessary, "Why, bless me, a cat!" or "Stap me, a small lion, what?" . . . These people show Superior Calm and I was sorry to find that my Ambassador – God rest his cat – belonged to the other sort. Two days later I found him alone in his office. He had sunk to his knees on his Bigelow, proffering a saucer of condensed milk to the cat and intoning, so help me

God, a litany which went something like *"Didums wazums drinkums pussums milkums"*. It was Basic English without the verbs – something no Ambassador should do because their knowledge of English is so frail. And there was Smoke with her first victim. She gave a slight acknowledgement of all this attention by uttering a small sound – the merest afterthought of a harmonium-on-sick-leave.

'I had a sudden feeling in the middle of my D. H. Lawrence that things had been put in motion which might well drag the Mission far out of its depth. I looked into those enormous china-blue eyes, I saw Polk-Mowbray grovelling on the carpet like a swami, and a sickening terror overcame me. "Here, let me pour, sir; you are spilling," I said automatically, taking the tin of condensed milk from his bemused hand. "Thank you," he gasped, and then catching at my sleeve, he added, "It smokes my cigar! It can practically talk, Antrobus!" The little creature took a lap or two in a sort of upper-class way and then stared at me in withering fashion. I stared back, not to be outdone – after all it was *my* Ambassador and, in a sense, *my* Chancery. Then, do you know what happened? *It winked!'*

Antrobus, overcome with the memory, swallowed his drink and gave a shiver. 'It actually winked, old boy. As I took the lift back to my office I felt as if Nameless Forces were at work in the Embassy. We would need all our *sang freud* – all our Upper Lip – before the dire business came to an end.'

'It all happened gradually, insidiously, for at first Smoke was content to enjoy adulation and respect from the whole Chancery while she or he or it settled in and began to feel at home. It is true that she sometimes puffed at Polk-Mowbray's cigar, which vastly amused everyone, but she didn't inhale, and she carried it off with an unimpaired dignity for such a small creature. She grew fast – who would not on a diet of grouse and caviare, with a touch of champagne in one's condensed milk? Wouldn't you?

'I think the first intimation I had of disruptive forces at work was when I rang H.E.'s office and a voice on the telephone responded to my quiet and courteous "Antrobus here, sir" with the words "Stinking fish!", uttered in a calm sweet voice, as if the phrase had been much deliberated upon. I was startled. "What's that?" I cried, and the voice answered: "You heard me, fishfinger. Stinking fish!" There was no doubt that my Ambassador had gone out of his mind. I rushed to his office and found him playing with string, making cats' cradles which the cat languidly undid with one claw while remaining half asleep on his desk. He swore that nobody had called, that the telephone had never rung! Fishfinger!

'Puzzled, I made my way back into the Chancery, only to find that each of the secretaries had the same tale to tell. In the skin of each festered some intellectual barb planted by whoever it was that had answered Polk-Mowbray's telephone. Young Bolinbroke had been called an inept prawn, while the Third Sec. (Games) had been compared to tadpole-spawn. We sat for a while comparing notes and, so to speak, licking our wounds. Bolinbroke had also been physically lacerated, while he was standing beside his Ambassador waiting for him to read a particularly moving and interesting despatch about the production of millet and rice in the Vulgarian South. Apparently without even waking, Smoke had drawn a razorblade lightly along his ankle before disappearing behind a curtain with an almost human chuckle. What was one to think? Diplomacy was one thing but cats was quite another. I did not see how we were going to combine the two.

'So it went on; the cat waxed in shining splendour and Polk-Mowbray began to lose his wadding. He neglected his duties, and spent all morning on the Bigelow rolling ping-pong balls around and having Smoke field them, which she did with the lissom dexterity of a Muhammad Ali. In spite of my misgivings, I had to admit that she was a great beauty with her sheeny soft coat, always freshly shampooed, and that great white archimandrite's tail which she carried like a standard when she moved forward. Or else, while listening to your conversation, allowed it to wave softly to and fro like some rare fern at the bottom of a tropical pool. The enormous blue Persian eyes were fresh as dew and sly as silk. In her general bearing she conveyed all the romance of old Ispahan . . . but I mustn't get carried away. I clung to my reason with both hands while I watched my poor

Ambassador sinking into mental debility, into second childhood, talking baby talk and cooing and caressing Smoke in a way that was terrible to behold.

'The matter began to preoccupy the Chancery and we wondered what sort of line we should take to counter this sinister influence. The first positive result of all this came when Polk-Mowbray's wife left for London to file suit for divorce, charging him with persistent mental cruelty verging on catatonia. I told him I was sorry to hear about this. But, running his fingers up and down the lustrous tail of this house-demon with a sickly voluptuousness, he only said, "*Pouf,* she is very sweet, Elsie, but she doesn't understand Smoke at all. Why, once she even tried to feed him – or her – tapioca. Smoke at once came to me and protested, didn't you, my *wazum didum buzzum?"*

'Worse was to come. I am trying to recount things in the right order – some of them I did not know at the time. When Polk-Mowbray came out of the nursing-home recovered from his brain fever, he told me the whole story. It was a case of gradual possession. One day, seated at his desk, he suddenly felt as if he were being observed, and raised his eyes to the window. Sure enough – at the top of the tall elm-tree in the garden outside was the cat. Smoke had surged up it and was staring through the Chancery windows. Their eyes met and a shiver went through him – never had he seen such a look. He had been born a generation too late for the Cheshire cat. Smoke smiled and gave a quiet laugh. He seemed, he said, to hear her talking inside his own head. It made him feel like a ventriloquist's dummy. "What are you doing up there?" he asked, and she answered laconically, "Lizards, silly." But this was not true. She was actually spying on Bolinbroke as he sat at his work. She had discovered that he kept white mice in his pockets and often, to relieve the tedium of so much finely fashioned diplomatic prose, he would let them run all over his desk.

'He was in a particular huff that week, for Polk-Mowbray had sent him a minute on the mauve minute-paper which is reserved for Friendly Admonitions. It read as follows: "About your prose style – Smoke says it is poor stuff. Try to avoid words like 'otiose' and 'serendipity' and you may improve. Otherwise . . ." You can imagine Bolinbroke's indignation. He spat fire as he showed it around Chancery and we realized that something would have to be done about that damned animal. As luck would have it Smoke had overreached herself that week. She had torn up a despatch and had sneaked into the cipher room where the head cipherine Miss Truscott had caught her messing groups about and sending messages of her own contriving to London. Naturally this was serious and Miss Truscott did not mince her words. "Your cat, sir, is responsible for all my corrupt groups this week and I am not prepared to be criticized for inefficiency by London when it is not my fault." Polk-Mowbray pouted and sulked but said he would talk to Smoke. But what could he do, poor drooling dip, against the Forces of Darkness? Moreover, what could *we* do – in the Chancery? Even Dovebasket was flummoxed. But the new BBC correspondent gave us an idea. He was old Trevor Hemlock – remember him? He of the gin-swept embrace? It was quite a simple thing really – they did it in the BBC when they wanted to get rid of someone. "Just overturn all your inkpots", he said, "and write a memorandum accusing the cat. That will do the trick." It was wonderfully simple and sophisticated as an idea – how had we not thought of it before? All inkpots were duly upset and Bolinbroke composed a scorching minute for H.E. From then on Smoke knew that there would be no quarter given.

'But meanwhile she had found some secret way into the cipher room and had started sending off homemade messages when poor Miss Truscott was not looking. Some of the results were calamitous – as when the Fishery Board found that it had ordered (without knowing it) thousands of tons of Vulgarian hake and cod for which they had no use. The result was Questions and riots. The fishmongers marched on London and scuffled with their MPs. "I am afraid Smoke has been rather naughty," said Polk-Mowbray, adding as usual his *didums wazums* while the cat purred and grinned in a loathsome way. "You know, sir," I said, "the whole Chancery is getting fearfully concerned. We think, sir, that you should rusticate your cat, send it back to Shropshire where you have your country seat. It should do well there, hunting pheasants and all that. But here . . . grave issues impend and we can't have the Secretary of State led astray by a mere cat." At this moment, so help me God, I saw Smoke turn around and glare at me with the face of the Devil himself. "Did you say *mere*?" she said, and I felt my knees tremble under me. Polk-Mowbray put out his hand to soothe her but she flounced her shoulders and uttered a slight hiss. "Tomorrow I issue my warnings," she said. We gazed at each other wildly, Polk-Mowbray and I. I think he realized in a dim and scattered way that he had been bewitched; his expression was one of almost pleading – as if he were saying, "For God's sake help me, Antrobus, before it is too late." But he could not actually say this, for Smoke sat there before him like a sultan and gazed contemptuously at me through half-closed eyes.

'Back in the Chancery they were waiting on tenterhooks for me to come. "I am afraid", I said, "it is war to the knife. The lights are going out all over Europe. Have you seen the latest cipher despatch about the fish?' They had. Their faces were drawn.

'At that moment Spole the Chancery Guard came into the room with the baskets bearing the latest despatches which had just come to hand. Among them was a pretty sharp query from the Secretary of State about the signatures appended to the last set of political despatches. It said: "The S. of S. begs to state that he has never seen FO despatches presented in such a singular form and signed in this slipshod manner."

'Slipshod was not the word. He had not realized that the papers had been signed, not by H.E., but by Smoke. She had dipped her paw into an ink pad and left an imprint of her right paw below every despatch. Under it she had added: "Smoke's mark." When I showed the protest and the despatches to H.E. he burst into tears and said: "What can I do? She talked me into it. I have become a catspaw, Antrobus. One can sink no lower." It was a painful sight, and I felt deeply sorry for his dilemma. Without a word – I did not want to add to his pain – I laid before him on his desk a short list of Cats' Homes for the Upper Classes which Bolinbroke had compiled from the Gotha. I did not want to rub it in. He mopped his eyes. "Is there no other way?" he asked, and I shook my head. "Never have so many owed so much to so few," I said. "Chancery is in a state of mutiny. Smoke, sir, must go."

'Sighing, Polk-Mowbray gazed out of the window at her, and I followed his gaze. She was at the top of the elm-tree, quietly, effortlessly, brilliantly, fielding sparrows as they passed. "I don't know how to break it to her," he said. "And do you think she'll be happy at the Sidcup home? It's true that Marcus Cheke keeps his Spooty there when he is away, so that there would be at least one FO cat to talk to. But it's a lonely and monastic life you propose for her, Antrobus." I knew how he felt, but I also knew we had to be firm. "Nevertheless . . ." I said – it's a word which has served me well in many a crisis. "I feel all strange," said Polk-Mowbray, "as if I were about to faint." I caught him as he tottered. "It's just the vapours," I said cheerfully, sure now that we had won our point. "They will pass and a new life will open before you." He shook his head. "I think after this terrible experience I need six weeks in a home." It was a good suggestion on the whole. He was obviously touched with acute brain fever and needed quiet. I resolved to make all the arrangements and I told him so. But first he had to take Smoke to her new home over the water, and cleanse his bosom of all this perilous stuff – I mean, corrupt groups and voices in the head. Who did he think he was, Evelyn Waugh? I left him gazing up into the tree with rather a daft air. I closed the door silently behind me. What a relief to feel we had won! A cheer went up in Chancery when I told them.'

'But there were many problems to be overcome as yet and Smoke knew it; it could not all be achieved in one day. For example, you can't just send a cat to a classy cats' home just like that – it's worse than Eton. You have to put her name down at birth – if possible even earlier, the moment morning sickness sets in. We had to compile a pedigree and a curriculum vitae for Smoke and to find her a sponsor. Well, we all set to work to invent a pedigree – they must have laughed down in hell to think of us slaving away at this document. We said that her great-grandmother had been the Personal Cat of the Empress of Russia and had escaped with her. She had been brought up in

Rome where the Pope blessed her and gave her the run of the Vatican because of the rats. Here she had served her apprentice-ship and had been sent *en poste* to the Vatican Mission in Vulgaria (as acting-proconsul Mice). Here she had become aware that among her ancestors there had been a British Ambassadorial cat, and it was he who had suggested . . . It was hard work but finally we got her past the board, thanks largely to an aunt of Polk-Mowbray's who ran the home. But the next thing was how to get her there – for she flatly declared that she was not going to leave Vulgaria until she had revenged herself on the Chancery. We read the omens and trembled, old boy. It was not long before she declared war. She left her visiting-card, so to speak, upon each desk. It was fiendishly clever. She had found the card index with the cards called "Character Appreciation", and she gave us a card each with her own personal appraisal of our characters. I must say it stung.

'On Bolinbroke's desk she left a dead field-mouse with its nose pointing towards him and the words "Only fit for a reproof and a sacking". Odgers got an insect and the words "Be warned!" In my case I got a dead goldfish and the words, "Total abjectness will never prevail."

'It was literally impossible to lay hands on her, though she never seemed to hurry. She just slid out of our grasp, drifting about like a wisp of smoke with a mischievous mandarin-like smirk on her pussy – if that's the word. Then she would swarm up a tree in the Embassy garden and start fielding sparrows with a bored and disenchanted air.

'We were almost at the end of our tether when Polk-Mowbray decided to call in the Secret Service. This was old Cedric Belfry who only went out at night, masked; Smoke had broken his code but had more or less left him alone. He was rather deaf and a chain-smoker. He received us in his office under the stairs. It was rather a depressing place; all the wheels and ratchets and presses and syringes – the whole torture outfit – were neatly draped in their covers of waxed canvas. Cedric wore a sort of Las Vegas eyeshade such as gamblers use. "You will have to shout," he said, which was quite amusing since the walls of his office were covered with Secret Service posters which said "Hark! Not a word!" and "Hist! Keep it dark!" and so on. We bellowed out our problem into his ear-trumpet and he gave it his mature consideration. At last he said: "In my view there is only one thing which will settle the matter and that is a Throstle-Whistle. No cat can withstand it." Polk-Mowbray said impatiently, "What the devil is a Throstle-Whistle?"

' "It is made specially for the Secret Service", said Cedric, "so that our agents can keep in touch with each other after dark. The sound is simply the love-call of a thrush, followed by a kind of plop such as a worm makes when it is tugged out of a lawn. It's fearfully ingenious. I am sure your cat would do a Pied Piper if it heard it, and specially the plop, it's so lifelike." He produced one of these things – which looked rather like an oboe – from his desk and did a sort of Indian love-call on it. "Do thrushes really do that when mating?" said Polk-Mowbray, who had never really learned to love and trust Cedric. "You bet your life," said our SS man. "When your cat hears that, all his deep hunting instincts will be aroused. He will follow the call. Once you have him in an old clothes basket it's money for jam. Do you see?"

' "Yes," said Polk-Mowbray, "I see. How many Throstle-Whistles will I need, would you say?" Cedric pondered. "I can give you two," he said at last. "That should do the trick."

'So they went about baiting the trap for Smoke, and in the greatest secrecy. Drage and Polk-Mowbray did a few rehearsals on the Throstle-Whistles – but they were careful to have their flourishes drowned by Bolinbroke on the grand piano. In this way the victim suspected nothing. At last the fatal dawn broke and the wandering Smoke heard the most delicious love-calls and plops coming from the dewy lawns of the Embassy. One group of calls came from the bushes by the drive where Drage crouched executing his share of the score in a worthy manner. Parked hard by was the Embassy Rolls with the blinds down; Polk-Mowbray crouched within ready to take up the theme when Drage fell silent. Inside the car the cocktail cabinet had been transformed by the addition of a large and comfortable theatrical hamper in which the cat was to cross the Channel. The fridge was full of catfood which the chauffeur was deputed to dish out to his passenger, as and when . . .

'As Smoke crossed the lawn in quite a mesmerized way towards the bushes, Drage's whistle fell silent. The animal halted and gazed about her in perplexity – no sign of worm or throstle, her gaze seemed to say. Then she spun round, for the delicious bulbul-like gurgle was coming from the Embassy Rolls now, from its shadowy interior. Surely the chauffeur could not be responsible for such a thing? Now if there is one thing that a cat cannot withstand it is curiosity – it begins to ache and throb with the desire to know. She hardly hesitated – her leap described a snowy parabola against the blue sky, and from inside the car came the noise of bolts shooting home. Those of us who had watched this operation from the Chancery window set up a ragged cheer. At last we had been delivered from Old Nick!'

'What a sad end,' I said, for I like cats. 'Antrobus, wasn't it rather caddish to lock her into an old cats' home like that? She should at least have stood trial or something.'

'It would have been the end of us, old man, and we knew it. Only the most determined action could and did save us. And by the way, though Smoke got life, in a manner of speaking, she made a wonderful thing of her new post – she regarded it like that. Moreover, the other FO cat exercised a wonderfully soothing influence over her during the first weeks of acclimatization. She had been psychoanalysed by Freud and was wonderfully relaxed. She took Smoke into her confidence and it was due to her that Smoke made such a good thing of her new life.

'You see, far from snuffing her out, she became a Sphere of Influence. The Russian Ambassador used to drop in for tea sometimes and get a lot of useful instruction. Once the Queen Mother called. And most young dips on their first posting would leave a card on her before setting off. It was in every way a roaring success, her new career. She posed for Dali and lent her face to every tin of Spoof, the new catfood, "A REALLY BALANCED FOOD, WHICH CAN CAUSE LEVITATION". Of course from time to time Smoke had hot flushes like any other ageing cat. Smoke poured from her ears and her tail sputtered with static. At such times they put her on the trapeze in the gym and she performed extraordinary feats. T. S. Eliot asked to meet her with a view to writing her into a cat-ode, but he found that she smelt disturbingly of brimstone, so he thought it wiser to desist.'

'It's an amazing end to a most equivocal career,' I said.

'In her end was her beginning, so to speak,' said Antrobus, smiling at distant memories of her reign of terror. 'But there is only one thing that worries me – they say that she is writing her memoirs. I hope to God . . .'

Antrobus at lunch in his club